MOTHS AND FLOWERS

MOTHS AND FLOWERS

The Writings of Samer Alshaibi, October 2, 1977 - May 1, 2006

SAMER ALSHAIBI

Artvamp Books

Contents

How this book came to be

In the winter of 2006, I sat in a hospital room with Samer and his family before he went into surgery to have his heart valve replaced. Too many drugs had taken their toll, and he was a kid in his twenties with the body of an elderly man. He'd been on and off heroin and cocaine, which had him spending stints in prison. He had been in prison when I met and married his brother, Usama. He and I became pen pals.

Samer lived with us when he got out, in a tiny closet-like bedroom of our teeny Chicago apartment. It was smaller than his jail cell had been, I think, but he was happy to be free. He was earnest, hopeful. I helped him apply for college at Columbia, and before long, he'd gotten a job at a Middle Eastern restaurant. His boss introduced him to a landlord willing to rent a charming old apartment to him for cheap. The whole building was occupied by artists. He met Sarah when we used his place as the set of our short film *The Amateurs,* and they became inseparable.

Bussing tables at a busy restaurant was backbreaking work, and because of his back pain, he ended up on painkillers. A doctor recommended by his boss prescribed opiates, no questions asked. That was the beginning of the end of Samer.

Already a former addict, he spiraled back into his old ways. He tried to get his brother and me involved in taking opiates, describing how to dissolve them in water and inject them via syringe rectally for the best effects. My gut clenched, my intuition screaming at this thought, and I adamantly refused. I could feel in that moment that Samer was headed for more trouble and might end up back in prison. I expressed my concern to him.

He never offered them to me again, but we would take late-night walks with Samer rambling on and on eloquently about every subject imaginable. We would meet for breakfast at a cheap little diner. I went on a trip with Sarah to New York, where we stayed at Richard Kern's place, and she did a shoot with him for *Purple Magazine*. The two of them saw us off when Usama and I traveled to Baghdad. We were close, but he didn't tell us when he graduated from pills to heroin.

He began selling vintage clothes from his apartment. His apartment was raided on suspicion of drug sales as well. They didn't find any. I suspect the maze-like flights of stairs from the front door to the apartment gave them ample time to get rid of any that might have been there.

Sitting in that hospital, his body bloated many times its normal size from heart failure, he asked me if I would make sure his writing – especially his still unfinished novel *Moths and Flowers*, got published if he died. I knew he was a talented writer from all our correspondence. He began *Moths and Flowers* on legal pads and whatever scraps of paper he could get in prison, and I had read bits and pieces. I agreed without hesitation.

He didn't die in surgery. The surgeon had told us, in cases

like his, he would likely start using again and would die young. He said this to Samer as well, which infuriated him. We all wanted him to be the exception and prove that doctor wrong just for spite. But we found out he was snorting heroin even while recovering in the hospital.

He went home. And he finally finished his parole. He was officially a free man, getting a college education and planning to open a vintage clothing shop. The relationship between his brother and him had been strained after we saw him with heroin in the hospital room, and we didn't hang out very often.

On May Day, standing on the rooftop of our new loft, Usama and I were shooting video of the mass of demonstrators parading down the street near the site of the Haymarket Riots. We got a phone call to come to the hospital. I brought my laptop to get some work done, as we thought he would be in there for a while again.

We were led to a room by the hospital clergy and found Sarah crouched like a cat on the stretcher next to Samer's body. I touched his arm, strange and clay-like, and I called his sister to alert the rest of the family.

Now it's time to make good on my promise. It's been many years. His brother and I are divorced with a 12-year-old kid who will never meet their uncle. Samer would have been 46 today. I've started my own imprint, Artvamp Books. Having a couple of publications under my belt, I knew what had to come next. I have left his writing mostly as-is with a few minor edits and fixed typos for clarity (with a little help from Goodrock for the first read-through). There is some repetition, which is intentional. A few pieces had been changed just enough to be interesting in their own right, and they show us Samer's process of continually shaping, adapting and perfecting his favorite bits. What follows are the poetic and often surreal peeks into one young man's mind who had a unique voice and an even more unique perspective.

Viola Voltairine
Samer's 46th Birthday
October 2, 2023

CANTO 1

LIVE SPECIMENS

I

Violet is Sleeping

Violet's breathing is so loud. I say things to her, not for her, but she still won't wake from her name solidly announced, not whispered. So as to not make a spectacle with jumping and screaming I rest my back against the wall, now behind the path of light from the lamp on the nightstand that lives next to the bed, that light now hitting a side of Violet's face, and that side now designing new shadows on an already dark side. I am not even that scared anymore, in here, but I just cannot go out there alone. She always wakes at the first utterance of a tremble in my voice when I wake like this and need to go pee. She knows I am sincerely horrified. Tonight, I am really not that frightened, just too paranoid and loyally stubborn to my paranoia to give in to thinking such things as "there is nothing out there."

I thought being in a room with no windows would ease some of this, but it has little to do with windows, and logic. I

2

even convinced her that we should have nothing in this room but the stand with the lamp, and our bed, because the objects, when looked at in a certain way, would appear as other things that bothered me. There is a lanky man with one leg as if it is a long penis-leg, and just a torso with no arms. He has a slanted hat like a farmer who has been bent over too long shucking corn and moving fast so his hat slipped, but he does not care, really. He is waiting for me to let him know that I know he is there. I do not know if he knows of the worm that has the pointiest ends that is actually above his slanted hat. This worm must move in convulsions because it spends large amounts of time in spasms, and then, sleep maybe. I do not know what they want to do to me, but they horrify me much. There are more, but these kind of live here these days. Possibly when it is time for something to happen between all of us the worm will spasm onto the farmer, but I do not want to even witness, or know of them moving from their respective spots, even at each other. It is a bit odd, the emptiness, just because of the size of the room; the rate of emptiness to size results in the value of hollowness. And a certain discovery recently made is about things severely hollow - fear echoes in them.

Pushing the top cover and sheet to her waist, I scrape my evenly pressing hand down her blinding white, red apple-flesh stomach and cup her sex, shoving my palm against and over its mouth; Violet's always clean, yet always stained, panties that happen to always be around her ankles when I have to be down there for some reason were there as usual on this night of a girl's heaviest sleep. Clenching a fist under the sheet, I softly rotated my knuckles on pinky finger knuckle axis, touching even her barely there wispy hair so lightly that

I thought of hovering, and things related to hovering. I was attempting a centripetal tickle. Her doing nothing says she feels nothing. And so my touching gets more aggressive as it gets more monotonous. I shrink all my limbs back to my own self, vanquished by the majestic apathy of sleep. Not because *I* am going to sleep, but because *she* is suckling on its funereal breast.

She is as before - a girl with slender branches for limbs, besmirched panties stretched thin around ankles from divergent legs, eyelids staring at the perfectly smooth yellow ceiling, sleeping deeply. There is a light beaming at the left side of her face so sharply, and seeming as if it is getting more concentrated, narrower, stronger, and brighter. Her ears are very big... no, no, not big... they just come out far, and so I call her monkey when that sort of talk is allowed, and proper, if time permits. Her long arms are at her side, but she really isn't that tall, long limbs and all. She has dainty thin brown hairs on her arm that are perfectly placed, appearing as if they are combed, but I do not believe that is what is happening with that. Parts of her back do not touch the bed because of the sway pushing it forward a bit, which is also pushing her belly up a bit. It looks cute on her, though. Her breasts are irreducibly juvenile... so small, and appear so hard, and maybe even violent... but to the touch they move as a firm cream wrapped with a flesh gauze. I wish her eyes were open so it would seem reasonable enough to tell you about them, and the things they can do. Violet's flesh is whitest, and if any other thing is said contrary to that, the thing said will exist its entire existence as a lie, even if something correct is supplemented.

This girl, Violet, is on a bed with a whitish blanket and red sheet up to her waist area, and it is where it is because of me; as is the light hitting her. I can affect some things. This bed is big enough for her to sleep in the manner I have exposed, and for me to sit next to her, watching, waiting. The wall my back is against is made of cement, but painted peachy pink, possibly to make one feel delightful as their skull shakes and shivers from brushing near it. If you knew where we lived, and entered our room now, you would be faced with the bottom of Violet's feet. Our bed is in the middle of the wall it is against.

There is nothing else to see here, unless you lifted up Violet's pillow, and mine; you would find a chrome .380 under hers, and a Quran that has a green cover and zips up under mine. We live in a building that has one entrance to three buildings, including ours, two exits, including our entrance, four stories, and it is rotting in the hallways. Our street is a main street that holds the same name and sicknesses as the city in which is the building, bed and Violet, the girl who is still sleeping. As you see, the only thing that has changed since the beginning is the movement of a light's path...no, that is a lie, its path was always the same, but where it obviously hits is different. I just knocked down the light onto the ground, and it's still on, and she doesn't care. I moved a blanket and sheet, a lamp, and my position to freeze my naked back against the peachy cement wall. I exaggerate a bit with the temperature of things, but never a thing else. The lamp looks ridiculous on its back and is shining on some flatness of the ceiling.

Violet, my monkey, has slightly tangled, tree-brown hair appearing as if it has been gently lain completely together, all strands touching, carpeting my entire pillow sweeping perfectly east. Her nose is of the blessed peasant blood, suggesting a possible aristocratic secret intrusion ago, quiet, resting comfortably, not leaping forward, tucked inward, trying to touch her forehead or her also blessed and narrow, but fleshy pink, upper lip. It is quite oily, though, as is apparent as she sleeps with it perpendicular to the hair that is floating eastward in up-and-down S movements traveling with the muezzins' calls to prayer from Jerusalem, Alexandria, Prague, and Istanbul, which was once christened Constantinople.

I had to pee badly. A time before this had happened, but it was with my mother as a child and she wouldn't go with me, so I peed in her bed, because that is where I slept. This has not been happening since those days years ago with mom, until Violet...until I loved her, and more importantly, until I knew positively that she loved me, adored me, liked me, became motherly and daughterly. I heard the word betrayal in my language, quit wandering and started to head in a definite direction. He may not arrive. She told me to always wake her if this happens and she will take me to the bathroom by hand; I always do. And she always does. She isn't now, though. Possibly, she is suffering where she is at right now and is trying to be with me, holding my hand to the bathroom, and turning the lights on in each room as we enter in order to show me what is, and isn't there. I miss her. I don't like it when she is sleeping, and I cannot be with her. I took the .380 from under her pillow and the Quran from mine. I turned the safety off and recited the last three verses of the Quran which all began with "Say" repeatedly as I entered each of the four rooms I had to pass, turning the light on pointing the gun everywhere I saw fit. I did pee, but I had to leave the

Quran outside of the bathroom because that is not allowed-
i.e., to have the word of Allah in places where people become
unclean; I did have the gun in my right hand, but I urinated
with the direct assistance of the left.

A piece of down could be seen above Violet's sweeping
hair. It was from my pillow. This feather wants to move away
from his home and go toward the lands he sees under my
head with the Bedouin eyes that sleep staring at Bedouin lids
for those eyes, revealing to the feather tales of all who have
come through the tents of my weathered fleshed great grand-
mothers and what they have seen. Maybe the tiny feather
wanted to see the glistening gold minaret's spire, a piercer of
all birds with broken wings faltering in flight; and the gold
needle and crescent moon perched on its tip reflecting the
sun, shine more of that light on the sun-darkened boys playing in sun-dried clothes on the sun-bleached dusty streets of
robed empires ruled by perfumed beards to thick mustaches
wearing tight fascist paramilitary garb, circa 1930.

Apparently, this piece of dirty white feather wanted to
visit, and possibly live, in some of those seen places. This is a
very normal and rational desire; we hear of it often. Logically,
he was traveling on the first thing he sensed going that way,
seeing that he may never have the chance again. And befittingly so, on the same pillow wherein he resided and first
learned of such places, Sarah's hair was lain suggesting flying
carpets and things similar. This was an imaginative feather.
She would never know anyway, I think, if it did take her
hair, because she was so detached from the goings on with it
anyway, and probably on it, too; and, amazingly, her hair was
only a pillow away, right next to her; it is not like it is being

used as a wig on a poor cancer patient some distance away. That feather was really looking at her hair and getting ideas about visiting somewhere, maybe even a place unbeknownst to me or my stupid nationalistic dreams.

I am bitter at times because I am aware of things, but because of this awareness, and definitely not bitterness, I remove the little strand of pillow stuffing from Violet's hair. My father is in the Near East now, and some things can even be difficult for him, but for a tiny feather - disastrous. Regardless, the politics have turned it into a more starker realistic West, which in context of living within will dominate the beauty of my honest dreams. Even if he goes somewhere else, how is a feather going to survive amongst the brutal children of this Earth. I placed him deep under the pillow-case so as to let it have a bit of a journey piercing its way back into the cloth barrier to reach fluffiness. The queer thing was that at the lifting of the feather Violet separated her fashionably black smeared lids and clearly said to me, "you pull my hair when you do that."

"Do what?," says I.

"Put your hands all on it and then you get up, or something, and then all your weight pushes on my hair and tugs my head...which is attached to my hair." She seemed to say the last words as a confirmation for herself rather than sarcasm toward me.

"I didn't do that...you didn't hear me?"

"Will you get me something to drink...I heard you, "you didn't do that," or something," she says as she makes herself appear helpless, turning her face opposite of mine and bringing knees to chest, not able to accept the place where she was suddenly thrown into by my lifting of a feather.

Of course I will get her a thing to drink; water is wonderful in moments as such. I love this thirsty girl a lot, and I also like her, I just have not decided whether she is good or bad. That does not matter, just a piece of information for reference. I bring her a small glass, so that if she drinks all of it, she will not get bloated and hurt her stomach, and I will eagerly move to go get her more, giving me an opportunity to convey something.

"Thanks," she says after sitting up and me arranging her pillows for her back to rest upon, and not feel the cold walls. She drinks all but a swallow, hands me the glass, and a smile delicately imprisoned with braces; with abrupt movements she twists her body toward the recently pillowed wall and yanks them back to their seeming destiny, throws the cover off of the majority of her upper-body leaving the sheet clinging to her knowingly and flops into a contorted position that denotes the strange shapes of comfort.

"I'm sweating...come to bed... now I have to take a shower today...how long have you been sitting there?...turn off the lamp," says she.

"I'm not hot; it must be where you're sleeping," says I.

I turn away from her, facing toward the lamp area lest she sweats more. I don't mind her sweat, really. It doesn't bother me, her sweat. It even makes me want to turn back around and molest her. I want her to not sweat if that is what she has decided that she definitely does not want. I know her, though. Even if she is shockingly intruded upon by me, she always appreciates random obscenity. I cannot say the same.

2

Twelve Instances

i.

Two days ago I was walking in the park because it was nice; and humans living in capitalist countries do these kind of things, yes? Two people were walking in front of me. Sarah was with me, as well. The one on the left drops a plastic/foil chip bag as if these chip bags naturally shed from his body as he moves in his environment at the threshold of a season. Surely this person does not molt as such. He did not use any force to shove this bag to the, yes, fairly sullied ground. And people, remember, my very, very young wife is with me and seeing all this. She is quite an impressionable young thing; we do not want her to think that this apathetic occurrence is "fine to do." This sweetest Sarah looks to me as soon as the innocent piece of trash hits concrete, and she puts her hand over her mouth to smother her gasp, huge-eyed and bones stretched on tiptoes to catch a glimpse from directly above the silvery inside of the bag. So I approve of her initial reaction but my own reaction is quite crucial at this moment.

I grasp the girl-Sarah's hand, as we were before this deviation but with a bit more connotation of something that holding hands already implies, and glide-walk to the stupid looking garbage and scoop it up severely smooth, without a hesitating step. I crumple it so as to make the commonly known empty chip bag noise. The left-side-bag-shedder glanced a glance with unease over his dumb back, and just then, in that fast peek he intended to give yet just to show that he knew what was going on and did not care, I made him look longer when I spun around doing an intimidating pirouette and sent the happy bag into where he was destined to go - the hardest, most metalest dumpster in the park.

In that moment, when the polluter saw me spin like that and throw that bag away, he was like, "shit...that motherfucka' is ill...pirouettin' like that and shit...next time I'm gonna' throw away some shit and be the cool motherfucka'!!"

2.

SILENT WEAPONS FOR QUIET WARS

I wake at the same time early in the morning irrespective of the amount, or quality, of previous sleep. Oh, and yes, sir, people of madam, I suppose you would feel neglected/denied/ really, quite upset with me, possibly even such a thing as violent, if I did not note the pertinent constants that would be perceived at the time of going to sleep, and at that repeated suspicious moment I wake. It is the body-Sarah, and the subsequent, seemingly subsequent, heat spilling from the girl's body; the poor girl, right? She says she has not a thought of her heat.

I wake with a monomaniac focus - sugar! I feel like I need it or else I cannot go back to sleep; and, I remain starving. As long as I sate the sugar craving I will no longer be hungry. I have checked all my levels lately with blood tests and the numbers do not even hint a whisper of diabetes. I don't know. I also grind my teeth, fiercely, and have nightly nightmares that have become routine in our bed-life. The nightmares are not seemingly nightmarish situations, or scenes, but the sense of horror and the fear which is imparted to me is beyond the scope of any of which I have heard.

Asleep, sssshhhh, quiet... upper torso is angrily yanked up from soft below, and furnace girl to left, GASPING, or a thing I do near what "SARAH?...SARAH?!" image so as to make me into the most tragic drippy wide-eyed, whimpering right angle, ever! Stuck in sustain because such immaculate, clean fears spill paranoia from nightmare onto bed.

I have a small Quran from my Tay-ta (grandmother) under two stacked pillows, that are on Sarah's side, and we say our prayers, mostly protective, which has helped much as of late. We keep it under that side because we can commonly be found with both heads atop said area. We cling to one another in sleep because our unconscious knows we are all really doomed.

3.
Even all the animals think us queer.

My sister flitted through town for a shoot, She is 4-5 months pregnant. We went to this new place that just opened up the street for breakfast. Wife is obsessing over a dog in an animal rescue shelter in Michigan. The dog's name is Nadia. Her old owner flung her out of the window of a moving vehicle when she was a very young puppy. She was then brought to the pound. The rescue shelter did not want her to be "put to sleep"; that is, killed. So they brought her to the shelter where they are now looking for a person, or people, who would like Nadia to live with them. Her leg is in bad shape from being thrown from a window; it may have to be amputated. She needs lots of medical care. Nadia is my favorite name, though. She is supposed to get along amiably with cats. We have a cat. His name is Television. We had three; Lilian and Eponine are their names, but they are with other people now.

I do not talk about it because that is what my mother tells me about these sorts of things.

We are going to Museums Monday, including the Skin Tight fashion exhibit at the MCA. Tomorrow, really today, is going to be pleasant. But I can not sleep.

I watched my wife sleep for a while as I usually do early this morning. I usually take pictures of this incredible occurrence for a certain reason but not this morning. It was more beautiful than many of the times before when I felt forced to leap for the camera and quietly shoot so as to sustain her bony pale frailness in warm peach light. This time I was stuck; I couldn't even remember where the camera was, and if I did, and if I could move, I would not possess the skill enough to decidedly take a picture.

Then a hollow wispy whispering vibration emanated from her fetal-curled up body. It moved in pulses toward me; a strobe holograph of her limp body being carried by fear toward me. Seeping into my forehead the ghost, her, wiggles it's still sleeping body through the brittle layers of my skull. Once in it twirls itself around almost giving me the same dizzying effect but I just fall because she was already spinning too fast for me to begin following her direction. I just fall and bounce my face-skin on the topside of a cat's paw.

4.

She sits on it, I wake, her body jumps and heaves, her ass stomps on my cock, her cunt twitches.

My wife, the monkey girl, gave me head a day ago. Her lips grip/clench my cock like she is hungry/STARVED and unabashedly glutting herself with it. She makes noises; first loud, then the soft whimper, but both are eager and begging - "NNNNNGGGGNNNNNMNMNMNHH?...nnnngh?" I was wondering why she didn't try to fuck seeing that it had been a couple days. She really likes to fuck, this monkey girl.

Later that night I lay to briefly rest. I wake to her slamming her ass down on my cock and convulsing/stomping/shoving herself against me. I fuck back. Her cunt twitches/quivers/gives. Slowing the violence, there are some lingering shoves. Of course the last flops of a seizure are startling seeing that you began to rest thinking that the epileptic's body was finally at rest. She isn't wearing makeup, but her hair is huge and touching everything everywhere. Would you believe that my wife hates white people? Disgusted by them, she is. I was just saying to her the other day, "baby, I know they look weird and shit but they cannot be born completely evil! You do not think they are evil when they are babies, yes? Are Jews white, baby?"

She put her head down so far that she was quite near face to face with the bottom of her front neck. Her neck is stretched thin, frail; a kind of thing that belongs only to the peasant aristocracy. I questioned her as to why. She said it was because we had not fucked in days! Now, like I said before, I do not know why she just didn't yank her head back away from my cock and stick it in her instead. That is a common thing for us; i.e., I stick it somewhere else after I withdraw from famined vacuum. Why not this again, huh? Why the waking aggression? Why hurl me so far from one place to another? After some time with her head down, eyeing her neck bottom, she races it up. She has something important to say! I know this because her top eyelashes curl down and her bottom eyelashes curl up meeting at the tips on each eye forming a protective cage.

She tells me that she, and some others, are the progeny of the Neanderthal. She tells me that cro-magnon did not kill all of them. I sense this has something to do with both hating white people and the eyelash cage.

DOOMISM: Believing in God but disliking God.

5.

The JAPANESE TONGUE CAMERA/ NEBRISTIC LOVE

The last attack I had lasted for an hour; it was something otherly, though. I remember thinking that I must die during this one because I am seeing things that a person that lives should not have seen. New forms, with numbers and letters. A violent ecstatic art.

New terms galvanize and popularize obscure activity.

Nebrism - to willfully be malicious to something to which you are inclined to be amiable.

This is usually practiced for ascetic reasons;to decline oneself the satisfactory joy felt from being friendly with that thing, and to possibly suffer as a result of nebrism.

My wife said something queer at the restaurant tonight. I was talking about how different dentists over the years have told me that my teeth get weak and sore due to me probably grinding my teeth while I sleep. I asked her if she had seen me do this.

"No," says she.

"I know I do it...because when I wake up sometimes...,"now sticking my tongue between my teeth,"ah goh ma tunh lie thi arlmo bininh ih oth!"

And then I also add, with tongue back where it feels proper, "there'llbea thin layer ofblood...andeverything...I know one day I'mgonna'wakeup...and it will be gone."

As sarcastic as this may seem I was serious. My wife was smiling with these glossed over inside her skull peering eyes twitching pupils at my face.

"What are you smiling at!" says I, trying to will myself to be enraged.

"I just was thinking of your little tongue, and how cute it is," says this dazed wife of mine, smile stretched a bit wider.

"What?!"

"You know, it's just so cute...your little tongue," giggling, giddy, delighted at the thought of the sight of my poor tongue, whether it be with me, or alone bitten off by my teeth which I now suspect of being in conspiracy with her for the purpose of the isolation of my tongue for her to easily withdraw from her hand-purse and be tickled silly.

6.

Waiting For Winter

Spent most of the day on a shoot with my wife with the photographer Mashu Kobayashi. We did the shoot at his condo but the next shoot he is doing at our place. Even if we end up buying a building or house I would still keep this place as a studio. We bid on an Araki original print but lost. The photographer today is going to put us in touch with somebody in Japan, though. Basketball, weights, running tomorrow.

7.

TAKE YOUR GUN OUT OF MY FACE.... BITCH!

6:30 A.M. AND MY FUCKING PHONE RINGS.

"hello?" SAYS I, KNOWING WHAT IT USUALLY MEANS WHEN IT SAYS 'PRIVATE NUMBER' ON THE CALLER IDENTIFICATION PAGE.

"HAMEER?" SAYS SOMEBODY, IRRITATEDLY, AUTHORITATIVELY.

"YES."

"THIS IS PAROLE AGENT BR___AJD," or something like that that I could not make out but definitely not my usual agent.

"Come down to your door and let me in," says this confident guy apparently at my door.

I tell my wife who is in bed that something is odd and not

right, but I am going to go down and let this guy in because I have an idea what would happen if I did not.

I also light a cigarette not knowing when it is I might be able to have one again. On my way down he calls again and says hurry up because it is cold outside. Now I definitely knew he wanted me out of the apartment fast in case I was preparing for something.

I open the door and I see about 10-12 plainclothes and uniformed officers in vests with weapons drawn including army-issue M-16 fully automatic rifles, and various other s.w.a.t. weapons.

"HAMEER?," a black man among them, who all look like a physically superior race of people due to their chest heaving vests, with the same voice as agent grumble grumble says to me.

"Yes." I already know what comes next so I just turn around so I am not mistakenly resisting and mistakenly shot in the fucking head by the white guy with the m-16 who seems pissed that I talk like a nerd or something who won't give him enough trouble for him to even draw his weapon.

"We're just gonna' cuff you for a minute," a semi-sweet semi-woman who appears from behind some crevice or wall, or wherever police live these days, says to me as they lock the primitive cuffs that I can get out of if I felt a need to do as such.

She said to the other officer that she was going to just put me in her car as they checked the place but I intervened telling them that they will never find my apartment because it is like a maze to get to it. They decided to take me, thank God, because I was just worried about my wife seeing all these people go through the house without me telling her it is alright. I wasn't really bothered but I just like to know what is going on; this was about the 10th time in my life I have woken up to fully automatic weapons in my face. My wife's face was an interesting one as we came through the door with me in cuffs and that damn big American gun pointed at my back. Those things do shoot quite well, though.

They did ask me where I slept and asked me if they could check it but I knew they could get a warrant issued anyway which would just delay everything and piss them off. Well, they do not need a warrant for the room that I sleep in but they do need a warrant for the house unless I let them in or they see contraband within sight in the apartment from the outside of the door, or window.

Some of the officers make small talk such as who is an artist as they look around the place and look frightened. Big American gun asked who the photographer was when he was in the kitchen with my wife which is a bit strange seeing that there is not an item around that would remotely allude him to it.

They look and find nothing. They are surprised. I thought I was done. I was not.

They tell my wife that I should be back in a couple of hours if everything is found to be "fine" at where they are taking me next. They put me in a patty wagon with a few others that this also happened to though I found out I was the only one whose house they searched. We were going to go get "dropped," piss tested - the analysis of urine in search of toxicological remnants of illegal drugs which is indicated by chemical reactions in the test and visibly made known by the changing, or not changing, of colors on a strip attached to the plastic jar with different colors for different substances.

It is a cold morning. Very cold, and the prisoners in the transporter next to, in front of, and around me were not seemingly affected by the weather. They were calculating how much time they will have to do upon returning to the joint. Old guys, young, black, latino, me. Mostly we were tired guys. And scared; I have never been cuffed and returned home within the day. We got there, got searched, had to take off my rings, chain that has my Islamic medallion and locket, belt, and shoelaces lest I am having a day a bit worse day than the others and I wrap those strings around my neck so that I may spill warm love on cold bitter cement floors where only the truly exhausted sleep.

Shortening the story -- the guy in front of me who takes his pee into the test jar says to the officer that he is clean and messes with nothing when he is asked. His test comes back positive for cocaine and he says he has never used cocaine in his life. He is lying. I know when people lie. He is still lying somewhere right now as I write and as you read. He will stop one day, though; I really think so.

They ask me the same question before my test, and after he asks me if I can go right now otherwise he said he can lock me up in a room for a while until I can. I tell him that I will be clean, as well. He hands me the jar that is difficult to hold over the toilet and pee into while you are firmly cuffed. He informs me that if I drop the bottle accidentally it qualifies for a drug positive result, which in turn qualifies you straight for prison, not rendezvousing in jail for a bit but straight to Stateville Correctional Center.

They would not tell me my results although I know I am clean; of course you still worry seeing that you have a girl who loves you intensely and would not function well if you were gone. I did not trust the guys who took my test because they almost screwed up in the beginning giving the cocaine positive man my paperwork and name; I thought since they showed everybody else their bottle as it turned colors and determined its constant negative answer why did they put me in a separate holding room cuffed to a steel bar behind my back and not let me see my own results? Finally somebody came in and brought me into a room for questioning by two ladies. All the women who kept on escorting me around to and fro holding me by the cuffs decided to frisk my chest and butt every time while asking me questions such as "how old are you?, you married? what you do?" All the women, especially one Latina was very upset that I was married and made it quite verbal with her girlfriends.

Of course my test was negative and it was such a big deal at the station that somebody was actually negative that I got all these congratulations and was sadly told that I was probably going to be their only negative for quite some time. That was wonderful but I wanted to go home. They asked me their questions trying to get me to talk about people in the joint. Afterward they took me back to the same room where I got cuffed again and waited for some time. Another guy was put in there, somebody who was in the wagon on the way there with me, and he told me that he was going back to the joint for a dirty piss result. He said he wanted to go and I said to him that he was bullshitting. His idea for wanting to go was stupid - something about if he goes in he will only have to do

7 more months or something but if he stays out he will still have about a year of parole...?

Stupid way to make yourself feel good for fucking up, but I wish him the best, really. Just after that they yelled for me and an officer gave me a ride home as he listened to his 50 cent album, hand on his "yaundastand me, ya dig!?" I am speaking of the thing we all really need, psychologically, socially, politically, spiritually - a gun. I am completely serious about that, too.

So now I am home and when I came in I frantically searched for my dainty dear to leap on.

It had sounded as if this building was being evacuated yet none of my neighbors poked their heads out to spy a single teflon vest or threaded barrel from which, if fate was to be so humorous, they may get shot at some date in the partly discernible future.

AT LEAST I CAN STILL SEE THE CURE, INTERPOL, MOGWAI, THE RAPTURES TONIGHT! ALSO, I HAVE COME INTO POSSESSION, ALMOST OF SOMETHING QUITE AMAZING BUT IT MUST BE IN MY HANDS BEFORE IT IS SPOKEN OF. MY WIFE GAVE ME THE NIKON D-70 FOR MY CAMERA BECAUSE I SAID I WANTED ONE OF MY OWN. ENOUGH WRITING AND GUNS AND CUFFS AND SHIT, BITCH.

8.

Been buying grapes lately but I will not no more. They make me feel disgusting and as if all is just a horrible, horrible thing. My wife makes a funny face at the thought of them in her mouth. She sticks out her tongue and says it is because of the skin. That is the okay thing to me, though. In prison you do not get stuff like grapes. Yeah, you do get things, but not grapes. I have had my fill. I haven't slept and I still have more work to do to complete this study but I think I will lay down now. My wife is in the bed with no clothes on. I am not going to fuck her or anything but she isn't wearing any. Her body is really sore.

9.

I just wrote an incredibly long story and mistakenly erased it. I saw an ex-girlfriend ride by on her bike yesterday and she looked at me and then pretended that she did not see me and my wife. We never even fucked, though. And we had to stop seeing each other because she wanted to fuck. She was trying to correctly follow the tenets of Islam, which I respect and understand as I, myself, am Muslim. We made Fajr salat to-gether the first night that we talked. That instructive thread of purple light skipped on the seam of the horizon making us stop what we were doing and turning our direction from each other to the sinks to make ablution for prayer. She did put her hands on my cock that first night, though. Days and weeks after that we began touching a bit more and I could actually feel the warmth emanating from between her without even touching it. She would call me and ask me questions regard-ing jurisprudence on certain subjects in Islam, and then she would sometimes ask me my own thoughts on interpretation, which she found a bit disturbing.

I had just gotten out of prison around a month earlier fin-ishing a 4 and a 1/2 year sentence. She asked me the first night we talked if I had been in prison. This bothered me, making me think that maybe the word "convict" was being whispered from my pores. We stopped seeing each other because there was this other person she was confused about and she and I knew that if we were alone one more time again we would really fuck hard. I met a girl at the time of the ending of that thing. She had braces and looked as if she was 12. We started talking because she was over at my just got empty apartment shooting a film and she was going through my boxes of books. There were many girls there but I had seen some modeling work of hers before, and her own photographic work, so I was waiting for her to knock. When she came in I couldn't even talk to her. Later when she was at my books I asked her if she liked to read and she said she loved books. That was really the only possession I had coming out of prison. We strangely started talking about Marx-Engels-Lenin-Smith, all this shit that I don't even think obtains our interest. After the shoot, she was still around and a few of us went to go and view a raw screening of the just-shot film where she plays an underage aspiring porn star with sore bones and an eyepatch protecting a poked eyeball. The movie is available at Earwax video. I couldn't talk to her because I was so fucking shy. I really liked her extremely proper manners and etiquette, sitting up straight in chairs and such. She was quiet, very quiet. But not shy. I liked her values, of what I could glean. She changed in front of everybody just upon entering the apartment. Well, the second time she changed. I lent her a sweater so that she would have to contact me to give it back. I got her number and said we should hang out. After a few tries I reached her and we set a time and day. Boy, I was nervous because I really liked her. I thought that maybe she was not interested because I thought that she would think I was different than I was because of the way I looked. Remember now, I just got out of the joint and I was the type of person who went outside on the yard, the only one out of a 120 inmates, at 8 in the morning in the middle of January just so that I could lift the frozen rusted weights. I was pretty big and thought that she would not like that muscle thing. Oh, and I have a lot of tattoos. I think she knew that I was nice, though.

I found out she was vegetarian so I took her to Chicago Diner, a very good vegan restaurant in Boys' town, that it took us hours to find. I told her I had been in prison on the way there and she acted a bit surprised but not really. I found out later that she already knew. We ate and went back to my apartment. While sitting on the couch I asked her if she had a boyfriend because I had heard that maybe she did, but nobody really knew seeing that nobody knows her. I then excused myself and went to the bathroom and brushed my teeth very fast. I came back out and kissed her.
She fucked me. That was a very nice thing to do, I thought. That was the first in over 5 years.

I will continue the story at next entry. Sorry for the uninteresting prosaic form but I am just kind of spilling it out in a just tell it manner so that I can see it myself. The interesting stuff is on the way. Oh, that sweater I had lent her - it would be the first in a long line of my favorite sweaters that she befittingly shrinks to her size and then suppresses her giddy smile when I tell her, "You might as well keep it now!" I like seeing my clothes on her anyway, though. Possibly a bit of homosexual narcissism. The her wearing my clothes thing, that is.

10.

INT. GROCERY STORE - DAY

Sarah is in the candy bar aisle with a gallon of milk in her hand. She is picking up various chocolates and inspecting them each. She steps back and surveys the whole section of chocolates studiously. She walks over to one a bit away and picks it up and studies it only to place it back exactly where she got it from. She goes to the register with her milk.

CLERK
You got a discount card?

SARAH
No.

CLERK
That'll be two twenty nine.

Sarah pulls out this folded bill and unravels it revealing another bill folded with it and some change; it is the exact amount. She hands it to the clerk and the clerk hands her the bag with the milk in it and she leaves.

EXT. BUS STOP - DAY

Sarah is standing up in front of the bus stop shelter holding the milk gallon by its handle with her stomach shoved a little forward and her butt pushed a bit back facing the boy sitting down on the shelter bench behind her. Her face is in the direction of the right though her eyes are peering to the left. The bus would come from the left.

BOY
Hey, girl...hey, girl, sit down, let me talk to you.

Sarah does not change her expression. She may hear him, she may think he is talking to somebody else; she may not have acknowledged it at all.

BOY
Damn, girl, I just want to say hi...

He is talking as he is walking toward her. He gets in front of her standing more or less on the curb. Sarah does not change the direction she is facing to the right but does redirect her eyes toward him.

Oh, so you see me now. You actin like you ain't hear me, I know you did...

SARAH
Did what?
Sarah speaks fast, beginning directly as he ends.

BOY
Hear me. Hear me call you over. You heard me. I ain't goin do nothing...I just want to talk to you.

SARAH
What did I do? Why do you want to talk to me?

BOY
I just thought you looked nice. I was sittin down and you was just standin there and you looked good so I was goin talk to you.

Sarah finally changes the direction of her face and looks down a little as she smiles exposing her braces that she attempts to cover with the milk gallon, and then her other hand all the while not wanting to seem that she is covering anything up.

BOY
See, that's what I'm sayin...ain't no need to be all scared and shit...you even smiling now...

The Boy puts his hand under her chin trying to get her to face him instead of smiling toward the curb. He is smiling in a smooth demeanor, acting quite coy. She remains smiling but constantly averting her face to one side or the other, or back down toward the curb. He is laughing light-heartedly at her seemingly shyness and aversion to his persistence at trying to get her to face him. She finally does it, but on her own more so than by the goading of his hand. CU of her head as her hair swings and eyes center on Boy as she faces him. She looks serious and tragic for a moment then begins to smile again, exposing teeth and trying to cover them up weakly with hand barely over that area.

BOY

Naa, you don't need to cover it up, it's pretty...I think it's pretty...stop all that shit...

He puts her hand that is trying to cover her mouth at her side and stays it there. She makes attempts to raise it again, but he just puts it back down. Nobody is smiling. He is looking intently at her and she is watching her hand being stopped incredulously. She stomps her foot lightly like a fed up child and he looks down at her feet and laughs at this. She looks at him, at a loss, half of her face is smiling now and the other side is straight. She has a look as "What are you going to do now with me?"

That's better...that looks right on you...

He starts to stroke her hair from front to back. She begins to move her head down again but he stops it fast lifting it back up fast and continues to stroke her hair. She looks at him again. He is smiling at her and she is smiling at him again. He twists a piece of her hair at the back and then palms the back of her head pulling her head a bit closer and then spits in her face toward her mouth while he contorts his face into a malicious grimace.

BOY

Dumb ass white bitch!...You a ugly as fuck, dumb as fuck, stupid ass ho!...

He is yelling this at her as he is walking away toward a group of two girls and one boy that are standing in front of a building behind the shelter, but a bit to one side. They are all laughing and boy 2 is bent over laughing as boy 1 reaches them. Boy 2 gives the pound to boy one as boy one is still looking at Sarah shaking his head in disbelief. Both of the girls are yelling things at her. Sarah has not wiped the spit off of her face; she is looking toward the direction of the group as one of the girls yells at her.

GIRL #1

...I don't know what the fuck you is looking' at but you goin get your shit split you keep starin', ho!...What, bitch, what?!

GIRL#2

Shit, she don't know...she best get her mothafuckin move on...

Girl 2 says this a bit quieter as if talking to herself.

Sarah turns her head slowly away from the group and makes sure the milk is okay. Sarah then returns to her original stance, head toward the right with eyes toward the left, but now her body is not as relaxed. Her torso is a bit more straight.

GIRL#1

...That's what the fuck I thought...

GIRL#2

She knows what's good for her, she ain't that motherfucking dumb, shit...

As if to herself again.

The bus comes and they all get on bus together. The group is talking about something else now. Girl 1 seems to be making fun of Girl 2, and Girl 2 seems to be just taking it. The boys are both laughing. Boy 1 shakes his head a lot and Boy 2 laughs in a silly manner. Sarah is just sitting in the front of the bus facing to the right, which is the front window, but looking to the left, back of the bus, where the group is sitting. She is not seeing as far as the group.

II.

She is just laying there, silent and sleeping. It has been a rough day for the girl-Sarah; that is too bad, really, just too bad. I like her to have a little tragedy, but in wondrous and gorgeous balloons. Ones that go up. And land in other places.

3

Vague History

The expectation of me and what I was to do had been decided before I knew I existed. The automatic power of being born in a certain land was to assist in ensuring my, and the rest of my family's, safety and well-being. Our people were under the spiteful, all-seeing eye watching and collecting data through the neighbors, friends and relatives who, in hope of averting the eye from themselves, assumed trustworthiness and then reported all. The paranoia of Baghdad is schizophrenic; one fears outsiders and themselves. My mother hauled me off inside her to a "feared outsider" in hopes of negating both the fears by becoming part of that outsider. I was born in Iowa City, Iowa. For reasons obscured, immediately after I was born, we had to return to Iraq amidst the country's war with Iran, my family's religious kin. The important task was done, though, I had papers proving my birth in this country. We were now waiting on time and a shrewd moment.

After sneaking through checkpoints in order to get us outside of the border we made it here. My father lived in various Arab countries, but not Iraq, for work. He came and visited us on occasion, but only for small periods at a time. We would go over to where he was too, occasionally for six-month periods. The Bedouin homeless gene was being confirmed in me. I never had to worry about much because I knew that we would probably leave from where the problem occurred. Escapism, I found its use. Nothing was serious enough to care that much about or become attached to because I created it as being so. I could not be that masochistic as to place my emotions on a thing from which I knew I would be torn. But the product of that was me being severely attached to things I thought I would always have -- my mother, foremost.

I felt alien in both cultures, my ancestral and my supposed boon-granting one -- American. I have two brothers and two sisters. My mother was by herself in this strange place trying to keep up with the confusing, rapidly growing new characteristics of my siblings. I began to learn how to use that as a way to avoid her all seeing eye, although my brothers and sisters, in hope of averting that eye themselves, collected and reported data to it. They were all older than me except one brother. They were in high school when I became noticed again. I was arrested at nine years old for destroying many people's houses, one about to be seemingly boring night. She was upset but she truly did not know how to correct such odd behavior whilst trying to keep control of a riotous household.

I did not worry about my dad seeing that he was this man who rarely made himself known.

I never got off probation or out of legal conflict since that first day of vandalism, captured. At eleven, when my father visited from abroad, he and my mother got into a serious fight that I saw. She divorced him after that. She had us living in fear of him kidnapping us and taking us back overseas. According to him, she cannot truly divorce him unless she was to do it through the Islamic system where it is quite hard for a woman to prove grounds for a divorce. It was only my little brother and I with my mom, jumping from place to place trying to avoid my supposed kidnapping father. She had to work, but she had to illegally because she did not have a green card. I avoided everything by rarely being home. At twelve my mother agreed to let my father have visitation with us for two weeks in this country. The night he arrived, we found a tape with my mother on it saying that she was leaving us, the kids, with my father to take overseas and not to look for her because we will not find her. I did not want to leave. My Bedouin gene had been dormant for a while. My little brother and I had to go anyway.

My father was still strange to me. He was nice, though. He sincerely wanted us. I wanted my mother to want us. I finally tracked down my mother from overseas and talked her into taking us back. Soon after I got back, I was sent away for more criminal acts. Soon after I got out, we moved to another state where things were to be better. After a year there I left home for good. I was fifteen. I traveled everywhere, hitch-hiking, train hopping, however there was a way to move. The gene was awakened. My family was worried but soon they learned how to tolerate it seeing that I was not doing it out of spite but more so for my own repulsion of being sedentary and idle.

Millions of things occurred during that period. I saw much, felt little. I would settle in places for small periods but only to have to leave because it was the cure against the insanity I would feel of being trapped. At one point I did settle for a while and forced myself to stay in the same city as my brother and sister. I was working and living this odd predictable life. I would confine the urge to leave and pretend it was an irrational ghost from my past. One week was bad. I already did not talk to anybody or see anybody, even family. I began to have fits of severe paranoia and almost went into states of unconsciousness. The nihilism I always knew I contained made itself surface. Or I pulled it from the depths of somewhere deep where it only suggested and then hid its amorphous tongue. I started doing random things with weapons. I would walk around my apartment with the weapon in circles and look out the peephole on my door. I saw much. I thought I saw much, therefore, I saw much. I would, at some moment, leave the apartment and do something unseen with lack of premeditation. Eventually I was caught and put away. I was put away for four and a half years. It did not bother me. I wanted that. I did most of my time in maximum security prisons due to the prison authorities feeling that the stuff I wrote in my diary was dangerous. It did not bother me much.

When I got out, I felt different than I ever had. I was still sure and resolute about little and remained opposed to being ideological toward anything. Except that. My girlfriend is quite fragile in many ways and the thing I want the most is to make her feel comfortable, desired and happy. I want to see beauty without having to possess it and alter it. If I have to create beautiful things in order to see it, I will and then release it. Sarah is beautiful but she wants me to possess her and would be uncomfortable any other way; so I will have her for her own sake and just watch everything else with her, as if she and I congealed. That is the only way I can possess a thing; i.e., if it watches with me. The movement gene has been quieted, seeing that it knows I cannot leave the city otherwise I will violate my legal stipulations and go back to prison. I have never conquered anything, just waded my way through.

CANTO 2

MOTHS AND FLOWERS

4

❦

Shayb

Zanib begat Asma, Asma begat Ghezwa, Ghezwa begat Intesar, Intesar begat Maha, and Maha begat the boy-child with wandering huge eyes in the Future land of Soft Cages. Wretched is how the beauty of the Eyed people since Zanib has occurred. The taste the Future land and its ancestral empires had, and still has, for the substance beneath the powdered waste Eyeds wandered upon instilled the cosmic paranoia of dispossession. The advanced weapon, Soft Cage, was far too shrewd of a device for the Eyeds to even arouse an idea of subversion. They tolerated and continued to submit.

The advent of Maha's boy-child began furtive talk wherever Eyeds wandered or slept. Of course, in the Future land it was of little significance seeing that few Futureds knew much about anything except to develop tastes for other's things, and, to sate themselves on that taste to glutinous excess. There were some Eyeds dwelling in the Future land besides Maha and the boy. Some were helping the Soft Cage gain faster and more access to more lands for their own perverse tastes in things Future and some, like Maha, were fulfilling their role in what all Eyeds have been waiting to come since Zanib. This boy was named Shayb, as it had to be.

The talk of him was inevitable seeing that he was the first Eyed with the gray hair since Zanib. At the time of the Civil Intifadah, the ruling family who were fighting were divided into two identifiable groups, one with gray hairs, one without. The ones without were quite a corrupt sort and eventually defeated, though still living amongst Eyeds. It is the progeny of the ones without that originally let the Soft Cage in to work its silent system. Zanib was the last one with the gray, and as she was tragically destroyed, so was the strength to rule and defend the ruling family. Until this new gray-haired Shayb scanned his huge eyes across the enemy land of the Soft Cage he was born on. With this single gray hair he demanded the adherence and respect, also trampled faith, of the Eyeds.

He did not regard much of this talk his mother would rant. He, growing up back and forth between Eyed land and Future land, became accustomed to the tastes of the Futureds and could not bear long periods of time in Eyed lands without being able to feed the way Futureds feed. His family and other Eyeds did not reproach him for such behavior because they understood that he had to have the realization himself. Through the realization he will have to look at himself and conquer the perverse appetite within him first giving him full insight on how it works and how it can be defeated. This time came with abrupt celerity but the battle of purging himself of the tastes would last longer than most thought they could wait.

Through relevant numbers and hidden arts that were anonymously placed in his path by Eyeds secretly watching over him he began to be aware of glitches in the system by which he lived and fed. He had no direction, though. He began to lash out at everybody around him until it became too much for him and he left in search...in search of what appeared to him to be nothing. He started to have an atavistic turn to the taste of wandering but on a concrete that is designed against such a system. He, still heavily impressed upon by the way of Futureds, viewed himself as they viewed him because of his new (but truly old) system of wandering. He could not exist under the fighting themes in his mind. He found an impermanent way to quiet them -- flower fumes.

By solely concentrating on the flower fumes and the process of acquiring them he was not buggered down with the weight of his genetic susceptibilities and the ones he grew with in a foreign land that was never truly foreign to him until now. But not only the Futured land was foreign to him, everything and everyone. The family and protectors, as sad as they were for him, knew that he had to reach this stage of galactic homelessness and amorphous identity before he could gravitate to where he is not only home, but found as well. It would still be longer, yet.

As Shayb inhaled and became lulled by the fumes traveling somewhere without apparent motion he came to know that he had been accompanied by someone for quite some time now. The closeness he had with this thing that was external to him had occurred so gradually that he never noticed its ascent into his life. This fellow wanderer was no other than flower fumes itself. He started to come to know that flower fumes has helped him destroy completely, with exception to occasional appearances by the dregs of societal influence, this amalgam of his mother's proclivities and the Soft Cage's trappings. He had no notion of what he was and was not creating one fast in order to be able to see the lands through an identity. All he desired was to be with his killer, flower fumes. This, flower fumes knew, was its time to violently leave him, spinning and twirling in the nowhere and nothing he thought himself to be before having realized he had been so consistently with fumes that he never noticed it due to lack of variation.

In proportion to the rate fumes began to disappear Shayb was making himself more apparent to the Futureds by what he was doing in order to keep fumes around. The Futureds decided that Shayb has made himself so apparent that all they could do to appease the other Futureds who demanded that such a Shayb as such should sit still in a Hard Cage for a time that is quite some is definitely put him there. Shayb felt this Cage to be a thing hostile, but knowing that he had to be somewhere if he could not be with fumes, he thought it befitting.

He came to understand that with the death and dis-appearance of his guide and killer, flower fumes, another identity death occurred within him. While fumes was killing other identities, it left its own. He will always desire fumes but he knows that it would not be the most proper thing to resurrect such a scent as fumes. What did start to occur is the linear atavistic motion in which Shayb moved. The history of the Eyeds was made known to him in proportion to the rate that the Futured tastes he saw in others, and that occasionally arose in his own part-self, appeared significantly disgusting. He, himself, even began to inform Futureds on how inherently repulsive they are but, as he once was accustomed to the incorrect tastes of an alien collective, the Futureds, they, too, can die some identity deaths and begin to see the Soft Cage, for much of the Cage's power depends upon its ability to go undetected. Shayb did realize later that this evangelical approach was a bit too eager and bigoted in its own form. Still, though, his portended possibilities were not made known to him by the many that knew of it. They could not tell him, yet.

After the Hard Cage decided that he should not remain there any longer than a certain period of time, he was let go after such a time. When he went to see his mother, Maha, who was begat by Intesar, he was under the impression that he had let her down and hurt her so severely that surely there would be a sense of resentment. It was not so. Yes, there definitely was some dismal emotion wafting about, but what it was may be a thing unidentifiable. She did begin to inform him on his gray hair and what is to be done with the power it holds. Shayb did not shrink at this, but rather, assumed a countenance bathed in vision. Whether it was the actual future or hallucination has not been made known as of yet to this scribbler of history, but one can agree that it is vision nonetheless.

5

⟨∞⟩

Porcelain Intifada

Asma walks into her room and closes the door, but does not shut it hard or soft, just closes it. She sets her backpack down on the floor and then sits on her bed and picks up the phone and dials a number that she seems to know quite well. It seems foreign to her. There seems to be this obscene pink blanketing the room. It is from the wallpaper, the carpet, and the comforter. There are toy animals stuffed with bulging plastic eyeballs festooned on the bed; some are more realistic than others. Shelves are lined with dolls seated in uniform order. All of these dolls seem to have smiles shoved on their faces.

The bed demands a jump in order to be where one is supposed to be on such a bed. It connotes a cheap princess in a rubber fairytale. There are diverse objects placed on various counters and dressers made of specific materials with random meaning for definitely no purpose in relation to their existence here in this place.

There are pictures on the wall. One might say posters. They have a predominant theme of boys who suggest postures and connotations of men who look like boys but do very manly things to girls who are no doubt women. These boys/men have on jeans and they are quite tight in addition to blond hair, or dark hair with blond highlights. There are plenty of these pictures. These boys/men are seemingly singers of seemingly songs. Who knows if Asma has ever looked at these boys/men agreeably. A window does occur in this room that she is in. Although, it has never truly occurred as a window due to the curtain never having been parted in order for it to serve its illusionary purposes. Asma is confident that she understands what is out there and she is confident that it is for the weak and cowardly. It is not that she is condemning the weak and cowardly, it is just that she is not that way so why would she participate in such a place as outside.

She is talking on the phone to somebody that does not excite her or bore her. She really would not let anybody have that effect on her anyway. Her mouth moves more rapidly as she simultaneously moves toward the act of ending this call. It is apparent that she was the one who ended this call. She does that sort of thing, not others. Many would not know that because they have no idea who this little girl is or what she does. And even the ones that do know her would not notice that she is always the one that ends the calls and not them. They would just say that she is a very pretty and sweet person because she most definitely is.

She does end that call, though, and now she is doing a

thing different than talking on the phone. She picks up her bag from the floor and puts it in the place that bags are supposed to go. She goes outside the room but shuts the door as she leaves. In that small moment when the door was open, a person, if that person was in that room, would hear noises that have no distinguishable creator. They are the autonomous sounds. So, a door opens, and the one who is in the room hears sounds such as vacuums sucking without vacuums sucking. She would have heard it.

When she enters again the sound is as blow-dryers blowing without blow-dryers blowing. The knowledge of these sounds sounding as a definite thing and knowing what that thing is, yet, knowing that it is not coming from its suggested creator gives it a hollow identity. What this means is that it cannot be stopped or hurt because no one knows where to attack. It has its own intelligence, as well. It definitely knows what to attack. Yes, a door can be shut on this thing or a method as such. Eventually the residue from being amidst its range will create a constant tone that one does not even detect. I suppose it does not matter if one does not detect it because then it cannot really bother one. Asma was carrying in a video camera and tripod when she re-entered.

Asma's mother yelled to her asking her what she was doing with the camera and Asma replied that she is making a videotape of herself. Her mother said that that was fine, but she should be careful lest anything break. Asma thanked her mother and her mother replied to her saying that she was quite welcome. Asma begins to set up the camera and faces it toward the edge of the bed that her feet usually dangle against when she lays on her bed without taking her shoes off. This dangling of the shoes on feet is for the purpose of a comforter such as the pink one that occurs on her bed not becoming filthy.

Truly it would not matter to Asma whether or not the comforter was pink, or even if it was a comforter at all. She just would not put her feet on a bed when there are shoes on her feet, even though her shoes are very clean.

While setting up the camera, she had difficulty getting a certain mechanism to work. The whole system relied on this one mechanism. She went to the manual for guidance. She was checking for differences or similarities between what she had done so far and what the book was telling her to do, in order to see if she was correct, which would mean the mechanism was broken. If the mechanism were broken it would mean that something was really wrong and the whole system would have to be rebuilt, or so they say. They probably just replace the mechanism and tell people the rebuild everything line so that they will regard the mechanism as a thing important to which care needs to be shown. She hoped very much that it was just herself that was wrong. She called to her dad to come in and take a look. He looked at it and said that one of the settings was switched to the wrong thing. So he switched it to where it was supposed to be. She thanked her father and he said that she was welcome. He left the room and she stayed in it.

She adjusted the height of the camera to make sure it would be right for what she needed as she looked through the viewfinder. She then pulled out her Quran from under her pillow that she sleeps on every night. She set it on top of the pillow. She left the room again. When she returned she was in a towel and her hair was wet probably because there was a towel wrapped about it. She took off her body towel first and started to dry herself with it. She did not look at herself once as she stood in front of the mirror drying off. This is not intentional, it is just that there really is no need to do such a thing ever unless a fly is in your eye, or as such. She made positive that she was dry before she stopped. She took her hair towel off and dried it as well. She then put her hijab back on but this time it was a new shade of black; it can be presumed that it was an entirely different covering. She did adjust this covering in the mirror to make sure none of her hair was showing.

She put on some clean panties but no bra because there is no reason for such a thing as that for such a girl as herself. A glimpse into her panty drawer will reveal plain colored underwear and cut comfortably, unlike the graven images of silly stuff strewn all over girls' panties. Her panties, she feels, is the only item in this room that makes her feel nice and neat. By understanding the color and shape of her panties one can peek into her psychology. These are the only item she bought herself in this room. She then draped herself in her prayer garb on top of her other clothes that she had just put on that she did not especially pay that much attention to, except that it matched somewhat. It is not that she is stating anything about herself in regarding fashion by matching, but she does not ever want to stand out so that is why she does a thing as such. She made her salat and then some extra ones that are not mandatory after that.

She went over to the camera and put in a tape. She pulled something out from underneath the bed that was linear and bendable in one direction that had some other clunky stuff stuck onto it. It was a dark color so it looked automatically like a foreign object that belonged to an adult. She set it on the bed, but behind her, obscuring it from the camera's lens. She grabbed her Quran and set it next to her and then adjusted the camera again a bit and pushed the record button.

"A-udhu-Billahi-Minash-shaytanir-Rajeem. Bismil-lahir-Rahmanir-Raheem. I seek refuge in Allah from shaytan the rejected enemy. In the name of Allah, the most Beneficent, the most Merciful. My name is Asma Sayed Mumtazi. I am thirteen years old. There is a lot I can say but I will try to be direct because as the Prophet's beloved follower, cousin and son-in-law said, "it is wiser to say less." I am not angry for myself but for God. I am only disgusted because I see what is happening to people who believe and even people who do not believe. I do not claim to know how God feels because that would be

Haram, that means sacrilegious, to the English speakers watching. I do feel from reading my Quran and just seeing the world that it is our duty as believers to enforce justice on this Earth. I feel God is watching us to see how we react to the corruption before He does. The Quran says that by the time that He responds it will be too late by then. It will be the end. These Zionists are apes, they will be despised and hated. That is what the Quran says it will do with them - turn them into apes, hated apes. What they are doing to us, and I say us because I am Palestinian, but more importantly a Muslimah...what they are doing to us is the same thing that happened to the Jewish people in Germany. They started with the ghettos then concentration camps. What were the signs

- curfews, checkpoints, shutting down businesses, stopping resources from going into the areas that needed them. These Jews, some of them, not all of them, learned these tactics from their Nazi masters and are doing it to us. They want to kill us all, I can see it in their faces. They look down on us more and more the poorer and dirtier we get. We get poorer and dirtier because we cannot get anything to change that. They want to just put us behind a wall and then if we do something they think is bad, they will fly their American Jets over our heads and kill some of us and tear off some limbs of some of us. It is always a lesson. They kill us in order to teach us something. We are supposed to accept it and then it will stop and we will go back to...to what? Checkpoints, curfews, borders, being poor, no schools because they shut them down or there is no money for them, no water to drink let alone to clean with because the average

Israeli family drinks around seven times, or more, water than the Palestinian, although our average size of the family is about seven to ten people and theirs is three. We will go back to not having a country that was robbed from us by a people we let in during World War two because nobody else would, and promised for doing so we would not be a British mandate anymore but our own country. We get to go back to being treated as rats by our other supposed

Arab neighbors who are all talk and just make deals with the United States who funded Israel with over eight billion this year alone. Saudi Arabia is the biggest snake...no, that is haram, a snake is a beautiful harmless creature from God who doesn't do anything except what it has to to survive; Saudi Arabia, where our beloved Prophet suffered and made safe a sacred home for us through years of body, mind and spirit pain. These kings and princes... vampires, who are there now are American prostitutes, Astighfur-Allah, may Allah forgive me. If they are comfortable, if anybody is at peace and comfortable right now in this world as there are corrupt people controlling our here and now and future and kids' future, then you are sinning. The Prophet said first try to stop it with your hands, meaning physically stop it if you are capable, if not that, then speak against it...if you can't do that for some reason, then speak against it in your mind, in your heart. Every Israeli is guilty. Not Jews, Israelis. Israelis say they are Jews but they are Zionists, and Zionists have to take over other people's homes in order for them to have a home. All of them are guilty. They all have to be in the military for a little while, even women. Their children are going to grow up and be our new and eviler oppressor, with an even more horrible idea about us because they remember every death we give them in their brain and add them up every night but celebrate every death they give us, even if they dropped a bomb on a house and there was just a baby in it. I could talk or I can do my part. The Quran says, about people who kick you out of your land, that you should kill them where you find them. Imam Ali, peace be upon him, says it is better to be below the ground than live subject to corrupt rulers above it. I know the Prophet said that a woman's jihad is raising children... which is very true... but we will not have any men or children if we all just sit and watch. I think life is a beautiful thing, I am not depressed...it is because I think life is beautiful, and because I love God that I must do my part, not as a girl...actually, yes, as a girl. As a girl who loves God more than anything else and cannot bear to sit and watch without acting. God has moved me and touched my heart to do this. As-Salamu-Alaykum-wa-Rahman-tu-Allah-wa-Barakatu. May Allah be with us all, and Insha-Allah, God willing, he will even tou...

"Asma?" Asma's little sister, Nadia, opens the door and asks.

"Yes, sweetie, I am right here." Asma reaches over and shuts off the camera.

"Will you walk me over to Fatima's house and drop me off? Mom says it's okay if you take me."

"Of course, little sweetie, give me a second to get ready." Asma picks up the odd object that was behind her on the bed and puts it on as a belt. It has square-like compartments stuffed with something going all around it. She puts a loose jacket on to cover the belt, and it is a bit chilly outside, so at least she will not be cold.

"What is that?" Nadia asks Asma.

"Just a weird belt," Asma was wondering if she just lied but went with it anyway.

"Let's go, sweetie," says Asma.

"Bye mom, bye dad," both the girls yelled.

"Bye," yells mom.

"Bye," yells dad.

6

Skips and Giggles

So sadly some girls touched me with such hardness that it shoved me to the dirty ground. The girls galloped off giggling without even viciously glancing at me, before the violent nudge, and after. I never did things to girls; I did not do things to any things, ever in my life. The only thing that was happening was Laylia and I holding each other's hand skipping at very reasonably paced hops. We were on our way to the Public Cottages of the Society of Snow Whores; a very wonderful place. I wasn't even really holding Laylia's hand because I did not know how to do it. I have never done that, and I did not know where to put certain fingers and such. Laylia took control and gripped her hand around my limp hand, and it probably looked more like a partly opened fist with my scrunched fingers sticking out of her grip though my thumb stayed out and ended up being able to use some pressure and make little tiny rubs on the top of her hand.

We were smiling, too, and it hurt our faces. Although the first time we talked was today at school break I know she is angry much and yells often; I have only seen a kind of grin on her face when a girl in class was informed by the Old Holy Lady that she needs to go home because her father and mother have been murdered. And she also has a pretend nice girl smile for old ladies I saw on this day when she got us out of class saying we were bleeding from our pisser holes. Laylia thinks it rude from God that we cannot read from the Quran and prostrate for Him while the blood is spilling out of girls. I understand Him and her, and like them both, and feel so bad when I cannot go into the Masjid because they say I am too filthy just from the dirt around plants and plant bugs. I have not really bled yet but she sincerely was and took me to the washroom where she took out a rolled up bloody brown cotton fluff from inside her and put it in my cunt that she had a hard time opening. I was embarrassed because her tights were just screaming white and she had womanly black lacy panties and she saw my spotted tights, just from plant dirt, and stupid dumb panties that were so small they made me have a big bulge like boys. She rolled up some fresh cotton for what she called her wound and told me that she put that in me because sometimes "the Holy Ladies are scummy untrusting fuck monsters that will meanly pry open the little legs of even a sweet nice girl like you, Elib." That is what she said to me but nobody was mean and they let us go although I did not lie at all because I did not say anything or put anything in me. Maybe they were nice because of that nice girl smile from Laylia.

I do not remember smiling before in my life, but I knew

how to do it. I felt naked and weakened doing it but I could not stop from doing it. Possibly that is why I was punished by the giggling girls. Laylia smiling was this dark sparkling thing; her lips were whiter than the usual bluish purple when stretched and she has two big teeth as a bunny rabbit may have that I glimpsed the bottom of because how could I not with them biting her thinner bottom lip. Her faint delicate hairs above her lips disappeared; I like the shade they add atop her usually tight eye shaped mouth. She is the palest and darkest thing. Her skin is darker than all girls here but there is a gray powdery film stretched all over that darkness. Possibly there is a white particle every fourth pore on her. Her diagonal wispy eyes were smiling even louder. When we left the forest path and began skipping I noticed Laylia's hair sticking out from her hijab; her hair did not lay and fall weak, it was strong and pointed toward any direction which it willed. I did not tell her about her hijab slowly falling off; I very much enjoyed watching her hair and the bloody tube inside me began to slip out somehow at around what seemed as the same rate as the hijab slipping.

I first saw the shove-me girls arm in arm, facing one another, yelling their giggles that were echoing off the low fluffy clouds possibly. They were two adolescent Snow-Whores skipping toward us at a queerly real speed from the horizon. Quickly getting closer and bouncing maniacally, and still facing one another, I could see that they were both smiling tenderly at each other though the one doused in freckles had a thick strand of white hair from one side and blue from the other shrouding her thin, wide mouth. The un-freckled Whore brutishly grazed me with her shoulder and tripped me with her shiny white buckled shoes, the shoes all the Whore girls wear, felling me to the spongy ground. I still had Laylia's lineless black pale palm in mine as I sat there with legs straight out and spread, and skirt umbrellaed over a bed of soggy mushrooms of which stuck its wet fleshy stems under my panties and at the beginning of both holes. I began to cry with my one hand still holding Laylia's and my other arm dangling on top of my ruffled skirt with palm up as Laylia stood empty gazed staring at the space in between the trees in the forest where the fast skippers vanished. Her grip was weak. Never would I imagine that her grip could be this vulnerable.

Just before we emerged from the forest path onto the stretch where I was assaulted by a skipping Whore child, I patted the healthy and hard tummy of the last tree we passed so as to make a gesture of regard for the trees, the pinks carpeting the forest floor, the queer sylvan creatures that occur there, and just all the wonderful things that happened there; I also touched that tree's stalk so that when I day-dream I may definitely know when the end occurred of the forest travels and when the "to the Snow Whores!" journey begins with joyous skipping on sloping plains of dewy hills. When we stepped out onto a moist, flat grassy incline I saw parallel hills just as ours to the east and west of us which also were attached to messy forests at the seemingly same place as ours. I looked behind me and followed the forest wall up to its tallest branch ends, making positive that some little mis-chievous, and bored, Giant child was not watching us from above and behind and snickering while he/she tampered with the scenery of Snow-Whore land. There was no Giant, or any of its eyes peering through the tangle of branches while it would have to be laying belly down behind us and forest to do. Laylia appeared as confused as I at the identical hills and forests behind them spread to each side of us as far as the last blurred green smear where we could not see beyond. We couldn't recall what was to each side of the hill every other time we had come here but we were positive it was not a thing as noticeable as this; we made a point to ask a Snow-Whore when at Public Cottage.

My puling and sobbing got louder and more pathetic by the whine waking Laylia from her comatosed and prolonged watching of the disappearance. She adjusted her blankness, let her hand drop from mine and dug a furrow in her forehead pointing to the point of escape for the skipper Whores.

"Elib? Are you fine, love, tell me, are you fine? I will go and get them and bring them, whatever you want, lovely...You know what types of things I will do to stupid girls! You know, yes?" Laylia looked down at me with her mouth stuck a bit open and still pointing in that direction. I really did not know, and knew the Snow Whore girls would yank her limbs apart showering themselves in palest black Laylia's brownish blood giggling for a moment and then bouncing off. I loved Laylia more than God now and do not want her torn apart. I told her that she should not go because something is not cor-rect here if a Snow Whore, even the girls, bounced into our people and did not notice. I am scared, possibly terrified.

7

❧

A Penis and a Cock

The brutal innocence of Laylia dampens the cunt. My neck hurt from wandering my gaze up high at the repetitive beauties in the trees. I do not like pain though that is what had to be known so that I may sickeningly gorge myself on these boys. This is the forest that is most dense with the most trees ever anywhere. And each tree is different. And at about the same height on almost each and every tree occurred two young brothers who were not twins but had such severe familial semblances that it suggested they were. The one with the dark lids blinking over reddened eyeballs was Sami. His body was besmirched. He must have been an active boy seeing that it was the sticky blood from his gory scratches and cuts, and other moistness, that bound him with the bark and bark-dust. His brother Wasi had the whitest eyes, softest skin, and deepest frown.

I do not have a memory of any cock before that of Wasi's.

I do not know where it was pointing to, but it was either many things or nothing. Any one thing that is noticeably dry must be thirsty. And also, anything that thin/emaciated, yet shatteringly stiff, must be malnourished, hungry, starving. The next penis floating in my head is Sami's. I know that I know very little about things but I think I am pretty good at knowing a thing's opposite, even though I do not know about any thing. These two tubes on this day that I saw them were strictly opposite the other, not in relation to space and place-ment in it but in the sense of form and the farthest distance one penis would have to travel in order to get to the other one's state. Sami, smile stretched beyond face and perched on the branch, ready to spring and pounce on birds, dangles a scrunched penis that shimmers so radiantly from its thick wet glaze it reflects the tops of the trees against the twilight emptiness of sky. After the blind spots faded from the bright dazzling droopiness between the boy's haunches, and owing my reawakening to the twitching insects of the early night and their noises, a tear fell silently to the forest floor from the tip of Sami's cock. Maybe it came out of that blinking little hole, or maybe it was just the wet cocoon collecting at that point in order to flee the boy's part so that it may grow. It did look like a thick drop, though.

I do not know if this is occurring on every tree with every Sami and Wasi, or just this one. Seeing that every tree is different, the lovely boys have to assume different positions relative to the trees' inconsistencies. There is a constant theme that exists, and that is Wasi straddling a thick branch, and Sami perched on a fragile one. And as I looked to some of the different pairs in other trees I could see that the cocks did the same thing in appearance, as did these children's faces. So, as long as the gravitational pull is the same, and I am sure it is because he is perched with thing drooping, the drop will occur.

Laylia was delighted as we entered the region of the brothers. As soon as she saw one of the pairs she ran to them giggling and trampling all those gorgeous pinks festooning the otherwise dirty dirt. Although the pinks seem to be placed randomly here and there she stomped and destroyed the majority on the way to the Sami and Wasi she wanted. Dainty pink petals torn with its spine shoved in on itself, mangled and contorted into a mass of darkened pink as a randomly sprinting girl's laughter echo bounces off many sated naked boys and many desperately desiring bare boys. The trees and plants refused to bounce her laughter off them because of either her carelessness, or deliberate malice; either way she should not be received well, they decided.

8

Letter to Asma, Pepsi Running

10/15/2004

Girls are different than boys. Uniforms say so. Asma is wearing her uniform, and I am wearing mine. Hers is a wondrous gray dress with thick straps that clasp with a button just above where I imagine lives the exact middle of her collar bone. I am only clothed in these horribly shapeless poly blended pants which demand even more attention by being fastened every morning, every piss and every shit, over the bottom of my decent-hearted faithful white short sleeve shirt. Yes, the shirt is of peasant stock...but it speaks with more distinction than the pants which attempt the puffy corpse sounds of the aristocracy though only to suffer even more rejection with its high visibility of desperation. The cut and fabric-simply said-inferior, lacking, needy, appalling, ugly, ridiculous, sickening and imparts the idea that any other sight is more desirable.

Though, Dear Asma,

I enjoy watching you in your dress. And Asma, I have only seen you in one form of dress so understand well that I am not confused at this moment and have conducted many various tests and equations until I happened upon the firmest result - I enjoy watching you in your dress. That is all, really, simply, to be said, though I will probably say a bit more. I mean, a thing as pretty as my enjoyment of the color communication of the usually dried blood from your scratched eczema on your knees peeking right below the bronze near leather dirt shine on the rim of your grayest pleated wool dress...Does this bother you? I watch you jump clutching the hands of your so somber friend, Renna, and when you realize that your gigantic smile has spilled out onto a laugh you cautiously dart a glance at Renna to see if she is still frowning, and when you realize that she is you are good enough a girl to find your own frown of sorts.

Oh, you know, Asma, those sorts of things are really good things, you know.

Yeah, they really are.

I just have not an idea what you must be wanting as you read this, or what your wearing right now...I mean, I really do not know these kinds of things, but if the dress stuff is a bad thing for you maybe I should borrow it for a bit and examine it, put it through some general scientific study equipment, and then maybe it will be not as magical as it is for me these days, and past. Oh, of course...I would lend you my pants and shirt during the duration of the loan. I would have it in no other manner.

What I really wanted to know, though, was do you remember when we played some number of years ago when we were even smaller, tinier? You just had a birthday I heard. We are both 14 now, but what does that mean for us both, not each? Remember now? You robbed me of my Pepsi drink and ran in the most longest strides down the whole street gasping for laughs so strangely and you would be made even more brilliant every six leaps as you and the moths glowed jaundice yellow perfectly beneath the streetlamps that seemed to brighten louder as our huge prison dimmed, time supposedly moved, and you still ran, giggling queerly, by yourself, but touching something of mine.

I ran for a little bit that night, after you. I liked it.

I did not care about the Pepsi, though I did want it when I first got it.

9

Asma's Flowers

Asma is in trouble. She wants the thing that will get her away from the thing she is getting. She originally started getting it because she wanted to want a thing and she heard that this thing would make her want it very much. Now she wants it so much and it is getting harder to get. She cannot stop wanting it that much because if she does not get it now, little tiny ants begin to bite her bones from the inside starting at her feet. It is not that she even really wants it, but, her body has to have it or else the little tiny ants will begin to have their way. It is a contract the ants have with the thing she is getting. The thing needs people to want it in order for it to exist, so, it lets an ant that likes to eat bones know the secret passage into their body if they do not get the thing in time. The ants have to leave once the person gets the thing though.

Asma knew she had to get the Weed. The Weed can get her away from the ants biting her bones while she withdraws from getting the thing she wants. She will still want the thing but, the Weed can give her the time she needs to stop wanting it without the ants biting her bones. The whole thing was a waste of her time. She would have never even wanted the Weed if she had never wanted the thing that would make her want it. If she can just get the Weed she can just sit around like she used to and think about how she does not want anything. She realized there is a new thing she wants - to want anything. There is a history.

Asma was ugly and pretty. Ugly, because that is what she thought others thought of her; pretty, because that is what she thought others thought of her at times, too. She did not know whether she wanted to be ugly or pretty. There were plenty of things Asma thought. She thought a lot. There were plenty of things Asma thought others were thinking about her. Asma began to get quite irritated with all the thoughts she was thinking. She would hear about others thinking less and feeling warm and nice. This began to sound like a thing desirable; that is, a thing others may desire.

She was not definite in her desiring such a thing as of yet because she did not want to choose to want a thing that was not possible to attain. That could lead to a problematic life. She truly did not want that. Well, she did not say that she did. There had to be a way to desire a thing and get it. She wanted to want something. That is what others did, wanted things. She would always see them moving and living because they said they wanted this thing or that thing, and sometimes, this thing and that thing. She thought that quite incredible; to be able to want more than one thing. That was truly something.

She heard of this thing, and saw others who have had it. It

was a thing that made you want it the more you have it. She thought that was wonderful. She, too, could have a thing that kept her moving and going and doing things. When people asked her what she was doing she could say she was getting this thing because she wanted it. Actually, she would not even have to say that she wanted it because if she was getting it they would obviously know it was because it was a thing she wanted. The thing was the Damned Flower.

She went to find a person who could help her obtain this Flower. That was not hard. Many people got the Damned Flower a lot because they wanted it, and the more you get it the more you want it. Asma wanted to get to the point where she wanted it so she could have a thing she wanted. Of course, the way one begins to want something is by liking it. That is why Asma never wanted any thing before, because she never liked any thing. She was worried she would not like it.

Quite expectedly, Asma truly did not like the Damned Flower as much as to want it with whole being. Others told her that she was not giving it a fair chance, that she should continue to get it regularly whilst being patient with it while it conjures its wonders on her. Asma, being the understanding girl that she is, in addition to not having anything else to do because she did not want anything, continued to smell the Damned Flower fumes. That is what you did with the Damned Flower once you got it -- you smelled the fumes and it would make you sleepy and nauseous. This was a sort of sleepy and nauseous one should enjoy, though. And true enough, after a time, it began to be a thing that she began to like, and befittingly subsequent, a thing she wanted.

She felt for the first time that she had an actual purpose

- to get this thing. The amazing thing about this Flower was that, unlike other things, once she got it, it made her want to get it more. So there was always something to do now, not like before when she would sit around and think and think without wanting to think about anything. It was not easy to keep on getting it.

After a time, she did not want to want it, she wanted to have it. The want became a true desire. She really wanted this thing. She would begin to feel a bit queer if she did not get it. She wondered if possibly she was better off just thinking and thinking without wanting anything at all.

It resulted in being a bit more than queer, that is, the feeling she felt when she would not smell the Damned Flower on time. She asked the Keeper of the Damned Flower what was it that she was feeling and it said that it was little tiny ants that would eat her bones were she to not smell the Damned Flower. Asma did not like this ant eating thing at all.

It was beginning to get very difficult to get the Keeper the thing it wanted in order that she could get the Flower she wanted. The ants sure would chew away and she really knew that the ants were a thing she definitely did not want. Many would tell her that she did not look pretty or ugly anymore, just wrong. If she smelled a lot of Flowers that day it really would not mean much though. She knew the many who were telling her these things were saying things important but she didn't have time to listen or think about it because she had to avoid the ants' biting which required her having to find a way to smell Flowers, which was very difficult and needed much.

She saw a fellow Damned Flower smeller one day start disappearing before her eyes after the smeller smelt a lot of Flowers. She asked other smellers about such things and they said it usually occurs though if somebody is there and sprinkles water on the disappearing body, while it is vanishing, you may be able to prevent it from disappearing, if the water finds the right spot where the person's body was so one will be able to see the water cover the non-visible area with substance. Asma did not want to disappear. This is one thing she realized she has always not wanted. That is the thing that has truly kept her moving when she thought she did not want anything. She discovered that she knows definitely what it is she does not want, it is knowing what she wants. If she does not want to disappear she knows that she wants to stay visible. Now she really wanted to get away from this Damned Flower and its ants that make sure she continues to get it.

One day, when Asma was confused about how to get away from the ants and the Damned Flower, she began talking out loud walking down the street. A child told her that he can help her. Asma did not know she was talking out loud so she asked how he knew. He said he heard her all the way down the street; he said never was a thing more apparent in his young life. She then asked him what was it that he knew that could help her. He told her about the Weed. This Weed kills anything Flower related and the bugs would die when they encountered it and then all the others would stay away after they sent their signals to the dead ones and got no answer. The Weed was only temporary. She would still have to make herself not want it. Well, not so much not want it, but not get it, eventually she will not want it when she thinks about it and thinks about all the stupid ants and all.

Asma sensed that there was something somber in the

child's face when he said that he would take her to go get the Weed. This child introduced himself as the Boy-Sarah. It was a strange journey through a blue land to get to the place where this Weed exists. The whole way through Asma began to love this Boy-Sarah more and more, yet, get sadder and sadder. The closer they got the weaker the Boy-Sarah became. The Boy-Sarah, at one point, turned around and told Asma he loved her as well. There was something else, though. The Boy-Sarah was really an Ant and by showing her where the Weed was he would die. Asma did not want to go any further but the Boy-Sarah insisted and even dragged her along at some point as she was yelling and crying. They reached a colorless land with the Weed in abundance.

The Boy-Sarah told her his last wish was to see her rub the Weed on her nose, for that is how one uses it, before he dies. She yelled that she did not want him to die but he insisted. She rubbed, and he died.

Asma has now gotten away from such flowers and barely even needs the Weed. She does not think about the Boy-Sarah too much because the Weed actually kills the thought of anything even ant related. She is moving quite purposefully with the idea that she knows she wants to be visible, to at least mirrors, and she likes to think about how she does not want anything at all, except to not want anything.

IO

Asma's Dreams

Asma has been having dreams. These dreams have been recurring since her early years as a very little girl. They all seem to have a constant theme, though. There is a boy, a little boy, who looks like her, with blackest hair and biggest eyes of a mucky green that suggests dirt. This boy is happy. Not happy because he is completely satisfied, but happy because he is not. This means he is happy with the amazing mystery and beauty of everything. He walks with a kaleidoscope around his neck on a chain. He grabs it and is in awe at the wonders he sees. Actually, Asma can see what he sees but never remembers any details. She cannot explain it but she knows that she saw it and that it was beautiful. Now, it was not any particular thing that was beautiful but, everything, the world, everyday things were just remarkable.

One thing she started to remember that was initially obscured from her was the light. It was bright. It was not blinding but actually revealing. It was so much brighter than the way things really were yet everything seemed correctly distinguished as if a correction of her vision had occurred. One day as she was looking through old photographs she saw herself as a little girl with a kaleidoscope. She noticed that she looked the same way as the boy does in the dreams; as she thought about it, she began to remember that everything *was* incredible through the kaleidoscope. Asmi, who seemed to go unnoticed by all except Asma, happened to suddenly appear. Asma said that she wants to find the kaleidoscope and look through it again; she wanted everything to appear like that again. Everything was beautiful, that is what is lost and needs to be regained. It was the beauty of something she could only see, wonder at, maybe touch, but never possess. So much has changed between then and now, though. She looked around the room and realized the stark difference between the emotion of the dream boy and her as a child in contrast to the dispassion of now.

She felt restless and dissatisfied, dissatisfied with being too easily satisfied. "What is the point of looking at anything, or doing anything if it doesn't make you feel good?" she asked Asmi.

" The point of the reality you are all living within is to not think about the point...it will hurt your eyes when you see the lack of beauty everything holds and it will hurt your mind when you realize the nothing you are feeling from what you see."

That did not make her feel any better. She started to deteriorate and weep. She wept for quite some time as Asmi stood still with his eyes shut. Finally she said "That is it...I am finding my kaleidoscope and the world will be beautiful...why did I ever stop using it, Asmi, why?"

"Everything became dull in it. It diminished, as with everything you do not need to use which decides its vanishing according to what is predominantly occupying your life. The colors and richness became obscured."

"How can that be? How could I not have a use for seeing everything as beautiful and feeling inspired and motivated from it? If I was motivated by it then wouldn't I rely on it?"

"You became too self-conscious and absorbed in the results of an action, an action such as who you will talk to, what will happen in an hour, and so on. You lost your innocence and began to be motivated by those results, therefore relying on it."

Asma knew there was something else; Asmi only answers a question in the context with which it is posed. She needed to know what she could do to regain that innocence, no, she thought, she should ask him simply how will she be able to see the beauty again through the kaleidoscope. And she did ask as such.

"You need a kaleidoscope."

No, that was not it, she thought. What diminished? What diminished! That was it. She asked a bit more antagonistic, "what diminished?"

"Light."

"Light. Light?"

"Light."

"But...there is light right now, there has always been the same light."

He said nothing seeing that he was not asked a thing. Asma,

realizing this, asked him a series of detailed questions regarding the disappearance of this light and got some answers. She discovered that the light has been slowly fading since she was a child because she and many others her age, and older, began to not have a use for looking through the kaleidoscope and seeing the world as beautiful and wondrous; they only needed to think about actions and the results of their actions, they became absorbed in such a world. Their new motivation was the result from the action they were going to do or the action they were actually doing. The light, which the kaleidoscope relied upon in order to be seen through, decided it would begin to not use all of its energy if people were not going to use it to see the world as beautiful. People still thought they were seeing beauty, but there was a difference. The beauty they saw was something weak and easily achieved, and the feeling they got from it was short lived. This was a beauty they could possess and consume unlike the massive narcotic effect of wonder and mystery the kaleidoscope's vision revealed. So the light faded more and more everyday. Nobody noticed such a thing due to it being so gradual. Cameras started using flashes during the daytime (nobody questioned it dismissing it as a new, evolved way to take a better photo), so all the pictures still were similar enough.

Asma needed light. She found her kaleidoscope. She had an idea. She went into a room that had special bright lights and turned them on and put her eyes to the kaleidoscope. What she saw definitely wasn't obscured this time. It was quite apparent. The light revealed too much with the wrong light. She saw the sickness and conflict in everything. Everything was warring, whether it was insects in the corner or cells fighting viruses in the body. All was violent struggle with the presence of negativity stemming from the realization that one must die in order for the conflict to end.

These sightings she felt compelled to frequent with the kaleidoscope started to be reflected in her actions. She began wars with others. She would fight and kill the relationships she was having with other people and family. She became very destructive and started to hurt everything she saw, from houses to trees and a piece of garbage on the ground to a dead leaf floating patiently in autumn. Her dreams began again. This informed her that something was wrong with what she was doing although she already sensed as such but did not have to reconcile with it on a nightly basis. Out of the nothingness Asmi appears and is seen standing with his eyes shut as usual.

"I know I am wrong...I don't know what happened, I went from wanting to see the world as beautiful to wanting to destroy it, and trying to do so. If it goes away because of people not using it wouldn't it come back by people wanting to use it?"

"No"

Asma realized that she did not know this thing's name to which she always poses questions. He was just a person and a voice now, but no name. Regardless, she needed to find a way to get an answer from him. If it goes away just because people do not use it must be a bit vain. Like all vain things it probably needs to really be convinced it is wanted and told all the time that it is needed. "Why did the kaleidoscope not work for me with the bright room?"

"Because the light was artificial and too bright. It was

harsh light. Everything you saw was true but too focused on which almost turns it into an untruth from exaggeration."

Asma decided that it would come back if it was sought out. She would seek it out very discriminately, though, in order to cater to its vanity. She would only look in certain places and avoid others. This is what she began to do.

She would only go to the places she remembered in the dream that she looked at and look and inspect every detail she could see with the kaleidoscope while avoiding other places that would yell "look at me, inspect me!" This weed would always do as such and Asma just ignored it. It would always tell her to get away from the flowers where she would sit and inspect in order to let the light know that it needed it to see this important thing. She began to feel more and more attached to the flower when one day it told her to pick it up and eat its smelly petals. It said that it would help her get what she was looking for no matter what it was. Her, being so desperate, did as such. It did make things seem beautiful and she felt quite good. There was one thing, though; it made her feel too satisfied and the light seemed to get much duller. How could everything seem so beautiful with me not even being able to see it. She thought it was better than nothing, and anyway, she could eat petals while she was getting the light to come back, which would be much better.

Asma began to feel less and less good and had to eat petals just to get back to the state she was in before she even began eating petals. Actually, it made things seem horrible if she did not eat any. They were becoming harder and harder to find and the flower leader would demand all sorts of things that became harder and harder for Asma to acquire. She would do very awful things to eat petals. She knew she was destroying herself but in order to just feel normally dissatisfied she had to eat the petals.

One day she took it too far and really did something quite vicious to get the petals. She had to hurt the weed, which was warning her in the first place, to appease the flower leader. A keeper of the weeds saw this and put Asma in a room out of which she could see very little, and nothing near the beautiful world that she was looking for.

She felt horrible and sick for some time because of not eating any petals. She did not care about anything in those moments. When she finally started to get better she realized that before she sees the world as beautiful she better understand what beauty is in herself without light. She was destroying herself knowingly with the flowers.

The problem was that she was now shut in a room by the keepers of the weeds. She wanted to leave so she could continue her looking and returning the light. A voice appeared. She knew the voice. It was the voice of the thing to which she always poses questions. She looked all around but only heard a voice clearing its throat.

"Hey, is that you?" she asked.

"Yes."

"Now why didn't it come back last time? The light...why didn't the light come back when I carefully looked for it and even wouldn't look at anything not important or listen to dumb people's words? Or did it come back? They're holding my kaleidoscope and I can't see anything here so tell me if it started to come back at least because it would have went away when I wasn't catering to its vanity."

"No, it has not returned at all. The reason nothing happened last time was because you were being too closed and narrow in your search for things to inspect. You need to see and inspect many things, important and not so important. And you must listen when things tell you to inspect when they know more about it. "

She did not know what to do about this situation she was in now, though. She got an idea, for once, from the voice on what she has to do. She felt more and more trapped. Never did any place look as dull as the weed keeper's lock-up. She did not hear from anybody, which she was not surprised about seeing that she was very bad when she was trying to destroy the world and then herself. The weed keeper people were getting more and more vicious to her. She didn't know if she would ever get out of this awful place. She called for the voice but she would get no reply; she did feel its presence. Now she was truly on her own.

She turned her survival mode on because of the horrible way in which she was treated. She felt that the world might be trying to destroy her now. The mundane dim world would have been better than this. She was tired of being pushed around so she fought back and let them know that she would not be treated as such. She did this by using and beckoning the things she had, and was now, inspecting. Yes, even in those seemingly meaningless things she could find something that had worth to see. She hoped the light was paying attention.

After some time they had to let her leave. She also realized that it was not the world who was wanting to hurt her but just some people who are just in the stage that she was in of wanting to destroy everything. By the time she left she had found value in many things and brought the light around herself. She got her kaleidoscope back and reveled in its vision. The more she looked, the more she realized that she had much more to inspect. Other people could see this light around her and some wanted it. She began to show them, as situations occurred, and only the little that she knew, how to attain their own distinct light. She also became aware of the light she once had as a child as being for children, and what they see through the kaleidoscope as being their own vision. Her new light was more complex and vast, and the vision she saw through her kaleidoscope made everything more distinct and separate. Now she could say something about what she saw but know it is a comment and not an explanation confining it to a meaning. She had to inspect and explain even better so that she could help others with turning their bland kaleidoscopic vision into a convoluted beautiful one.

11

Laylia's Blackened Skin

Laying on my too big bed, I started reading a book in a language I like but do not know about orchids. Looking at the pictures I decided they are gorgeously vulgar. A thing I may be. With their scooping lips and orderly random petals deceiving all the little unsuspecting bugs to fly about and breed for them. Possibly the bugs know and they are just nice like that. Or maybe they do not care and have not much else to do at that moment. Maybe it feels just as good as bug to bug hump. Stupid bugs. Asma blankly staring at the mirror brushing her blank hair. That girl is something to fear but I am not afraid of her. I probably love everything or do not know what not liking is. I am positive I could dart over to Asma right now and kiss her much on her dead, wet lips. Yanking her head back by her brushed hair. I do touch her when I am agitated with love for her and I slip into her bed because she is my sister and I love her. She will mutter with cheek pressed to the edge of the bed. I hope she is thinking of me or a thing like me.

"What do you think of orchids? Do you think them gorgeous?"

"Orchids? The flower, Elib?"

"Yes, orchids, flowers, more than flowers."

"Let me see." I show her pictures of a few that if I were a bug I would definitely hump even if I knew they were orchids.

"They're nice, I don't know why you say 'gorgeous', but they are nice flowers."

"How about not as flowers? How about as animals, people, or parts of people? What if you looked down your panties and saw one of those?"-- I, pointing to a voluptuous specimen.

" Mmm, it is hard to say, Elib... maybe it would be nice in my hair; what if you saw what is 'down your panties' sitting on a stem where an orchid sits?"-- she flicks my cunt like a drunk old penis beast putting on a show for his mates, all chortling and me bashfully blushing with slave contempt.

"Ouch, do not do that, Asma! What if I hit you there?"

"I would bind you to your huge 'gorgeous' bed with rough 'gorgeous' ropes and let the mangy dogs lick you with their dirty tongues all over your orchid, drenching your smelly petals and crumpling them all up!"

"No you would not!," says I.

Even if she did let that happen to me I believe she would feel bad afterward and do something to make me feel better; somehow. She probably does not believe that she would. I lay on my bed and she on hers.

"If you are upset with me, then here, hit mine... as hard as you wish," says she.

" I do not want to hit yours Asma, just please do not do it again."

"Yes, Elib, yes; if it is what you wish." Odd where she gets the impetus to speak from , for I know her mind is dead and body impressionably supple, susceptible to its molder.

While turning the lamp around toward the wall so Asma could sleep I was flooded with sadness when I espied a still ladybug on the lip of the casing under the scalding bulb's heat. Death, death, death, oh lord, such a death! Asma would feign concern for my sake but it would end up being more harmful to the dead ladybug if the girl was roused. Its wings took on an albino tint, unless it was a living albino, and they were spread in wanting flight. Surely the heat could not have been as powerful as to torch it to death or immobility before it could flee. No, that is not what happened.

Possibly, it died of old age and its body was mutilated by the heat after it died; wings spread as an "I was a ladybug once" gesture. If it was living , in good health , and it wanted to flee when sensing the glass bulb's death rays it could have just flapped its spotted wings and found refuge in some cool, healthy crevice. Perhaps it was tired of having to flap and leave cozy little niches every moment a despot decides it wants a little light or some fire to make its mother dinner. Perhaps it was challenging the forced and imposed biology it was given.

It said to the bulb, " I do not have to leave at the advent of your incendiary glory... I will hang about a little longer than usual , then leave." And its wings became crisp, flimsy legs brittle. Maybe it was just sick of the beetle way.

"Go ahead light, burn me and my adorable tinyness to

pointless ashes! Alas! I am alone in this too tight universe amongst poor roaches and monomaniac ants. Rarely do I encounter other strays of my own kind... and if I do, they treat me as a foreigner with their freshly pollinated bodies shunning my domicile dusty thorax. Then they leave, and I stay. What could I possibly do out there with them? Yes, this is wretched, but this is the wretched I bear because I am aware of the hostile vastness that is wrought when one leaves their allowed place. Those other beetles are not jolly, they are just comfortable. At least I am truly miserable. Even if I tried to assimilate back into the dewy stalks and soft piles on magnetic flowers I would still be aware of this place, hence -- cringing from the otherness intruding. So this light that burns so bright, burns too bright to see. Hot! Hot! AAAGHH! Ouch! It is hot! It burns!" That tragedy is tragic indeed.

I must do something with this fast frying dead integument. I could incinerate it properly seeing that that may have been its intentions initially. It seems a little too queer to bury anything. I will eat it and say, "Bismi-Lahir-Rahmanir-Raheem" for it, and I, and it will be the good thing for us. While trying to get it out of the lamp I under-gauge my monstrous hand and send it diving under the bed. I cannot remove it without making a clatter and waking my nothing sister whom I do not want to bother; I will continue tomorrow. It may be nice for it to just decay under the bed or possibly feed its peasant, but friendly neighboring, ants. "Bismi-Lahir-Rahmanir-Raheem."

I love God often. In his coy wrath and mercy. If I clearly envisage the Prophet

(may peace and blessings be upon him) I cry. And his grandson Husayn (peace be unto him) with his foreseen, willful tragedy at Kerbala. One by one they advanced toward that whorish army and conquered them by dying, as the weak baby gains sympathy by inviting the incubus to violate its softness and make it pure. Yes, Husayn (peace be unto him) wins with his head in the enemy's hands uplifted. His eyes still supplicating the sole war determinant in the ether to proceed with what must occur next.

And Ali ibn Abu Talib (peace be unto him,) Husayn's father wed to the Sacred Daughter of the Prophet , being decapitated in Koofa while praying. Such a kafiruun shall expect the tortures of something otherly that I cannot say but take delight in knowing it will happen. Who is better in punishment than He who compels the toady angels to rip half of the face off alternately with hooks while the other side heals? That is really nothing, though, just language. We can do much. If we must. Bloody, the deaths of the House of the Prophet. The pool of Abundance in the Jannah incarnadined by them spurred by my and their pretty Allah.

A tinier girl than my present smallness I stretched on the bed my playful, scabby limbs. I implored this god for a micro act for a micro girl. A very fair request if one knows what fair is. Or cares. There and then heavy epileptic jolts shook those limbs.

A superfluous answer for a tiny query and a puny girl, I might say. I will say.

Did He not consider how fragile I was and how huge I know He must be?

Laylia's palest black skin suggested eclipses and funerals. I thought my cunt should slide the whole area of the girl she owns. It feels so wonderful and isolated to be wanted for touch. I sat on the friendly bench next to the postern every recreational period eating my fruit and drinking my milk. But because of the demanded fast in Ramadhan I just sat and made my eyes appear as if they were looking at the negative space between girls playing rather than the girls themselves. Difficult with them skipping and leaping all about like hyper particles.

Laylia intruded my space watching with her suspiciously non-intrusive heat.

"I am sitting here because a boy last night was hellishly loud, I live with uttering with that froggish hellishness eating my damn mind.

You have to go to reading class next , yes?"

"I thought we all have to go?"-- I , assuming a normal voice.

"Yes we all must go but I am bleeding now so I cannot read so I sit in back and bleed and watch and think wretched "--she, joyous with down crestfallen eye at last words.

"Oh , so you do not have to make Salat or any such thing as that?"

"No, nothing with that glorious joy as if bitter jinns were flooding out of me huh? Ha ha they're dumb. You bled?"

My mouth has nothing to say, but do not worry, I am not frightened. She fills a sound gap that is only a gap because of her.

"You have those big huge pathetic eyes so beautiful I want them. Wow, imagine with your hair out. That would be some-thing I want." That is what she said.

I would have loved to give her some eyes then and there; I do not want to have a thing somebody else wants. It saddens me wholly. I let her know what I want from her.

"My sister Asma has bled some I think , and my mom bleeds, and some other people I have seen. I enjoy watching your skin; I have watched it before but never this close. I would like to see where it is that skin is made like yours."

"It is different than yours -- here." She grabbed my wrist and placed the face of my stupid hand against her different cheek. Hot cheek, punishable, magnetic wet, needy. She released my wrist and as a sad, lorn ladybug she looked as if she was saying "please look at the pretty I am , you can have me , just don't stomp on me. You must take me lest I get stomped."

My fingers heard the ladybug and are not as rude as to stop grazing her cheek from mouth corner to Hijab edge. The veiled sisters were thieving glances out of their naked obvious eyes. Of course , in their veiled huddle apart. Laylia saw my concern and killed the sad ladybug by turning her head, imparting the sacrilegious girl's face to them forcing their eyes to the trampled dirt. I knew her mastery over lowly me and the veiled sisters.

"They shouldn't look at anything save thick black cloth ...those damned harlots... nasties. Do you talk to them? You should not, it is not a good thing to do.

"Nobody talks to me, even veiled sisters. Why are they wearing those veils, Laylia? Those veils, Laylia?"

"Because they are alive and ugly, little beast." That is what she said.

I have seen one of the veiled girls unveiled in the washroom. She was sickeningly beautiful. Laylia is not a liar, though. Laylia asked me if I would join her some time when school-time ended. I said I would.

Before playtime ceased, Laylia requested that I go with her

to the bathroom. There, she extracted a tubular blood soaked cloth from her cunt and placed it on a window-sill where no window occurs. She handed me a fresh roll of gauze and ordered me to wind it into a cylinder, tightly. I started doing what she wanted of me. She was bestriding the toilet raising her skirt and shoving some mature mauve panties down over her sparkling stockings and scooping water from toilet onto ruddy slit.

12

Crotch Divining

My mother is an alchemist. She can metamorphose petty daemons into vengeful Gods and stupid crickets into hyper butterflies. Although they are still vengeful daemons and hyper crickets. She was not disgusted by my portended possibilities, rather, she felt chosen, grateful. Iblis himself acquired a seraph's body and wrapped its gargantuan pinions around her, stifling mother with the noxious heavenly stench and all crushing her silly bones with the imposed pressure of its span tightening, dry humping her with its asexual pelvis. She liked that. She contains a deference to things seemingly more powerful, different, formidable than what she knows. And mind you she knows much. And like me, and me like her, she is galaxies afar from being an ingrate.

My mom tells me my significant nativity was bestowed on her from a talent descending from our progenitors. Its advent is said to be obscure, but there are stories. My mother and our familial patriarchs of yore prophesy by reading the telltale patterns spilled from the vagina onto its environs after a full undisturbed menstrual period. The receptor of the divination must erase all the hair in relevant regions such as holes and inner-thighs when anticipating, or at first signs of, a gush for clarity's sake. My mother attempts clarity where clarity can be achieved, especially the temporal proceedings of a hallowed rite. My mother tells the women they cannot wash the affected area during the bleeding and they must make their niyah (intentions) to the Black Succulent Girl for a foretelling spill at the foretaste or inception of a droplet. They must not wear panties or under-garments. No intrusion into nether cavities. No cleaning after any discharges from holes. It is mustahab (recommended, not obligatory) that they should think about the color Black; not objects black but Black as Black is. Black for clots. The women predominately express difficulties with the Black meditation. I understand the frustration of such a thing. When the time arrives for a reading the woman will be ushered to the small house behind the garden that is reserved and maintained for such a hairless cunt cabala. The garden is very beautiful too if one enjoys those things. The woman will be told to remove all her clothes with exception to stockings and jihab. Woman is placed on special chair with leg braces and fetters for ankles, wrist and neck made from lambskin. Following quite naturally-- woman is fettered. The braces move vertical and horizontal; depending on the woman's stature her legs are raised and spread to a specified degree. This is for clarity. The legs must be lifted as high as it takes to espy the smeared and oftentimes irritably puffed holes. Most are bespattered with young acne resulting from the week-old shave. Some feign embarrassment for the stench billowing from their fragile bodies. It only matters a trifle because my mother is quick to allay them by imparting an idea of it being a religious scent that one who is "clean heart" should revere as an attunement to a thing otherly. "Like sour flowers from the clean God," she says with twitching black ballerina eyes scanning the ether and palms tempted to cup breasts but withheld from contact by her sharp nipples' fear of a gratifying pleasure. My mother does venerate the smell; it can be inferred by the briskness her gait assumes amongst God flowers contrasted with the diffidence she wears in the sterile, whitewashed cosmos.

She does not read me because she says she cannot see me, "beloved Elib," in a clear way. This upsets me and tinges places with pangs of jealousy seeing that Asma is read quite often. She says she does not worry about Asma so it is not the same. "Asma is different habibti ... I do not sit and say 'ya Allah, where is Asma? Why Asma do this? What Asma will do?' Only I worry too much about you ... Asma is good girl and you are good girl too ... but always make me say 'oh, God' ... you understand habibti? Maybe if I read for you I see something not there ... because I too worry too much. Who care? Why you want me to read for? What happen for you want me to read for you? You want me to ? I do it for you if you want. You don't need it, baby ... if you good nothing bad come, and if it come I take it away. You good girl, nothing bad will happen. Remember, when you very little girl everybody say 'aahhh, very pretty, kulish halwa' ... you remember, Elib? Still very pretty, you know, yes?" We are close, though, and we do things together that Asma does not.

Often, my mother will beckon me to the divining shack as she is positioned on the jointed chair with neck and ankles gyved by dyed lambskin manacles. Maybe because she knew I felt outcast from the ancient rite, she would take my menses rag and stuff it in her mouth. She would then gesticulate to me so that I should pee into the lovely porcelain chalice my grandmother gave her when she became thirteen. Momentarily dropping the rag from her mouth she would remind me to throw the fresh contents in the chalice all amongst her like-mine little body. With "angry eye and crazy you have, Elib!", but only when I see her eyelids shut. Sometimes I miss the cue and she will mutter through her teeth clenching the acrid, bitter muzzle, "naa, naaa,aa," from which I decipher as "now, now," and I, who feels gratefully chosen by a thing different than what I am boorishly accustomed to, oblige with the fury she requests. Willy-nilly, and to my surprise, I occasionally send down a drop of inoffensive offal right onto the daisy ornamented tile floor or in my panties, and by serendipity I find a thing to do with it. I am also allowed to spit until my palate is grey with desiccation irrespective of any cues she may mumble through bloody rags. Obviously, I am more than just an observer and tool in baroque pantomime that is solely mother and I. Why my mom wants me to masquerade myself with "angry eye" while her eyelids meet idly can only be answered as her desiring my nourished catharsis alongside hers. We involve all the elemental properties of a reading and more, but embellish it with our love and discard the cold impersonal between reader and readee. And, as is apparent, no Asma.

My mother waxes all her hair down there and exhorts

Asma and I to do so as well; although, sometimes I do not and sometimes I will not. I have always sensed that she is bitter toward her excessive vulva. While she is chair bound, doused and gagged, and occasionally besmirched, she will grip an isolated phallus and impale the sullen, dangling graveyard with the vehemence of my father and the frustrations of his failures. Although the cadence differs, the wet plunging threnody pictures itself as a slimy, squishy slug pulling its malleable little body up a coarse concrete hill wending its way to a dull apex. My father is a dead man.

13

Moths and Flowers

I went to watch the sewer-grate girl walk three steps length-wise and four tiny steps adjacent to the width of the oblong cavity that says "SewerGrate." Her bare Lilliputian feet, susceptible to all the filth that hovers and falls from things above onto the porous ground that we stomp arrogantly with our rigid foot-fortifications, escape vitreous, smooth, impervious. I did not see her toes move. No longer shall I believe that her feet even touch the sullied ground.

They do levitate the height of a baby moth standing upright on its hind legs, tummy exposed. The only doubt lies in the inaction of not laying my head with ear to concrete so as to give me the vantage view needed to exact this not phantasm. I am not rude. And she has been kind enough to appear stolid to my stares at her circumambulations around the striated vacuum where waste is, giving me a thing wonderful for my horrid, big eyes. I gaze, not gawk, yes. I do try to stand at the same place when I am compelled to go there so as to not disrupt the dizzy calm. It is difficult because the only fixed objects are sewer-grate girl and sewer-grate. Crossing the threshold whence I came-- Behold!--a comfortably bleak stretch, smears graduating to resolute horizons terminating in vanishing points that promise the same funeral of the senses were I to skip thither.

At toes' first touch on the girl besprinkled tract the inter-mezzo takes twenty-two metrical steps to come upon, or seemingly upon because it is hard to be positive, my mez-zanine proper where the pink-clad girl's ambulatory floating can be enjoyed detached. After I see her it becomes possible to leave the plane. A quantitatively expressed tramp is revealed to me when it is time for me to know so I may cross back over the twinkling, conterminous border. Revealed numbers vary. Little choice in regard to motion when numbers are implanted; I am too frightened to resist as of yet. The presence of terror when fleeing is not imparted by her but numbers may be. It is from without us twain. She has been only most passively kind and receptive of our tacitly agreed distance in tableau. She must be foreign to such a bitter grate, her being all pink and queerly wafting about. I do not move forward implying motion toward her, or the hole she circles, past my respective spot(s); I do move sideways or retrograde for escape from ominous feeling that is not from her or I. Nasty invisible that compels me to uncouthly flit somewhere otherly from girl; sympathetic girl giving the numbers so at least I may return whence I began.

She wears the pink sticky material stained with soot, menses and shit. Not ancient pink but urgent, obscene pink.

I suppose she affects her significant stools devoid of my eyes. I worry about it because I would be simply horrified if I were the cause impelling her to possess something she should dispel. Her little pink shorts and strangling bodice strangling her gaunt pallor will never harmonize with that sepulchral skin and death-brown tress in a classical sense but she makes her statement well. I do see her pee and bleed from her tiny bulge through the pink. Bulging from a reaching out not an intruding in.

She is smaller than me but both our breasts are irreducibly juvenile. Hers are harder. Adamantine but destructible. Maybe ours touching would be as metal scraping ice-- hers metal, mine ice. I understand the distension in her cunt as being familial with my little bump. My bulge more bitter, brutal; hers detached, wondrous object, gooey curio. Maybe ours touching is as when blood floats on milk; hers milk, mine blood. And the line of separation/connection is the bitterness I contain toward something otherly and hers the insouciance at something she owns but will not own. And like mine hers should be grazed and rigorously rubbed not pierced, irrupted. My eyes big and round, hers short and slitty.

The violent pink uninterrupted tracts on those shorts effete to gossamer between her holes. Yes, a withering cloth track, I will say beginning, from the linear dent betwixt her rear impressed by the pressure imposed from her squalid little humps. It extends to and vanishes within the neglected, supple fleshland that suggests a third chamber-- the limbo span a louse must traverse from the harsh plexus of pubic confusion to the delicate wisps of hair adorning the asshole; the Red and Black ant's zenith. A forsaken nexus where chafed pink struggles by tenuous threads latching on to the left and right moments of flaccid pink inner thighs so as to not be subdued into the amassing collective absence of crotch. Suddenly reemerging from the quasi-moth hostility onto the aplenty whole pink calm it is only distressed by a tiny bump who says "cunt." And eventually-- synthesis with smiling pink facade made viable by the flatness of her boyish pelvis. A thing said about pink in grey is that it is death in truth. And pink circling holes-- a beacon lest you trample and fall.

I have a mother, too. I like her but I do not know whether she is good or bad. Maybe she is a bit disconcerted that I am so filthy. She tells me when other people say I am filthy but she has never said that I am filthy. I am a bit filthy. She does say that there is a smell. She never attributes the smell to any-thing, but I do. I would wash my body. It would be horrible if she said that I have an ill smell. She says she cares nothing of the hordes that sniff me, that she will tell them to go and sniff their own miserable offspring if they want horrendous scents. She says she will tell them that, if I like. And then she asks me if she should say as such.

Elabathoria is my name. It is diminutive of Elizabeth Bathory the Blood Batheress of Hungary. I am referred to as Elib; I do not refer to myself as either. It would be quite perverse to refer to myself, yes. In my mother's mouth the taste of Bathory persisted while in my mom's tummy I did as well. My mom knows things as such, especially the metallic taste of Bathory in her mouth as growing me depends on the nourishment of such a mouth. It bespoke of the possibilities of such a child. The Bathorian possibilities. Not another banal vampiric baby, as all are. Mother, Salomi, thought much of painful virgins; parthenogenetic notions of herself became pandemic in Salomi, garnished by the memory of my father lulled by things that lull. The father thought contributed much to her ideas of autonomous insemination seeing that the lullaby objects estranged him from significant semen while, and after, pounding Salomi mom with stiff, angry but dismally dry cock.

Midwife Maryam and the servants swear by their huge humble God that Madame Salomi in a somnambulistic stroll sauntered into their sleep chamber unnoticed and loomed over their weary sleeping bodies with an exquisite twist of the lips and a nasty blade who says "nothing nice." On one definitely remembered day my nihilistic sister, Asma, walked to the library with steps and stomps that appeared as she read my poor gestating mom a book about Countess Bathory the mother woman lady's skin's sanguinary thirst being slaked by servant and peasant women. I suspect my sister used a tone chummy with revelation to goad my mother's sense of awe. Asma is nasty as such.

My mother is an alchemist. She can metamorphose petty daemons into vengeful Gods and stupid crickets into hyper butterflies. Although they are still vengeful daemons and hyper crickets. She was not disgusted by my portended possibilities, rather, she felt chosen, grateful. Iblis himself acquired a seraph's body and wrapped its gargantuan pinions around her, stifling mother with the noxious heavenly stench and all crushing her silly bones with the imposed pressure of its span tightening, dry humping her with its asexual pelvis. She liked that. She contains a deference to things seemingly more powerful, different, formidable than what she knows. And mind you she knows much. And like me, and me like her, she is galaxies afar from being an ingrate.

My mom tells me my significant nativity was bestowed on her from a talent descending from our progenitors. Its advent is said to be obscure, but there are stories. My mother and our familial patriarchs of yore prophesy by reading the telltale patterns spilled from the vagina onto its environs after a full undisturbed menstrual period. The receptor of the divination must erase all the hair in relevant regions such as holes and inner-thighs when anticipating, or at first signs of, a gush for clarity's sake. My mother attempts clarity where clarity can be achieved, especially the temporal proceedings of a hallowed rite. My mother tells the women they cannot wash the affected area during the bleeding and they must make their niyah (intentions) to the Black Succulent Girl for a foretelling spill at the foretaste or inception of a droplet. They must not wear panties or under-garments. No intrusion into nether cavities. No cleaning after any discharges from holes. It is mustahab (recommended, not obligatory) that they should think about the color Black; not objects black but Black as Black is. Black for clots. The woman predominately express difficulties with the Black meditation. I understand the frustration of such a thing. When the time arrives for a reading the woman will be ushered to the small house behind the garden that is reserved and maintained for such a hairless cunt cabala. The garden is very beautiful too if one enjoys those things. The woman will be told to remove all her clothes with exception to stockings and jihab. Woman is placed on a special chair with leg braces and fetters for ankles, wrist and neck made from lambskin. Following quite naturally-- woman is fettered. The braces move vertical and horizontal; depending on the woman's stature her legs are raised and spread to a specified degree. This is for clarity. The legs must be lifted as high as it takes to espy the smeared and oftentimes irritably puffed holes. Most are bespattered with young acne resulting from the week old shave. Some feign embarrassment for the stench billowing from their fragile bodies. It only matters a trifle because my mother is quick to allay them by imparting an idea of it being a religious scent that one who is "clean heart" should revere as an attunement to a thing otherly. "Like sour flowers from the clean God," she says with twitching black ballerina eyes scanning the ether and palms tempted to cup breasts but withheld from contact by her sharp nipples' fear of a gratifying pleasure. My mother does venerate the smell; it can be inferred by the briskness her gait assumes amongst God flowers contrasted with the diffidence she wears in the sterile, whitewashed cosmos.

She does not read me because she says she cannot see me, "beloved Elib," in a clear way. This upsets me and tinges places with pangs of jealousy seeing that Asma is read quite often. She says she does not worry about Asma so it is not the same. "Asma is different habibti ... I not sit and say 'ya Allah, where is Asma? Why Asma do this? What Asma will do?' Only I worry too much about you ... Asma is good girl and you are good girl too ... but always make me say 'oh, God' ... you understand habibti? Maybe if I read for you I see something not there ... because I too worry too much. Who care? Why you want me to read for? What happen for you want me to read for you? You want me to? I do it for you if you want. You don't need it, baby ... if you good nothing bad come, and if it come I take it away. You good girl, nothing bad will happen. Remember, when you very little girl everybody say 'aahhh, very pretty, kulish halwa' ... you remember, Elib? Still very pretty, you know, yes?"

We are close, though, and we do things together that Asma does not.

Often, my mother will beckon me to the divining shack as she is positioned on the jointed chair with neck and ankles gyved by dyed lambskin manacles. Maybe because she knew I felt outcast from the ancient rite, she would take my menses rag and stuff it in her mouth. She would then gesticulate to me so that I should pee into the lovely porcelain chalice my grandmother gave her when she became thirteen. Momentarily dropping the rag from her mouth she would remind me to throw the fresh contents in the chalice all amongst her like-mine little body. With "angry eye and crazy you have, Elib!", but only when I see her eyelids shut. Sometimes I miss the cue and she will mutter through her teeth clenching the acrid, bitter muzzle, "naa, naaa,aa," from which I decipher as "now, now," and I, who feels gratefully chosen by a thing different than what I am boorishly accustomed to, oblige with the fury she requests. Willy-nilly, and to my surprise, I occasionally send down a drop of inoffensive offal right onto the daisy ornamented tile floor or in my panties, and by serendipity I find a thing to do with it. I am also allowed to spit until my palate is grey with desiccation irrespective of any cues she may mumble through bloody rags. Obviously, I am more than just an observer and tool in a baroque pantomime that is solely mother and I. Why my mom wants me to masquerade myself with "angry eye" while her eyelids meet idly can only be answered as her desiring my nourished catharsis alongside hers. We involve all the elemental properties of a reading and more, but embellish it with our love and discard the cold impersonal between reader and readee. And, as is apparent, no Asma.

My mother waxes all her hair down there and exhorts Asma and I to do so as well; although, sometimes do not and sometimes I will not. I have always sensed that she is bitter toward her excessive vulva. While she is chair bound, doused and gagged, and occasionally besmirched, she will grip an isolated phallus and impale the sullen, dangling graveyard with the vehemence of my father and the frustrations of his failures. Although the cadence differs, the wet plunging threnody pictures itself as a slimy, squishy slug pulling its malleable little body up a coarse concrete hill wending its way to a dull apex. My father is a dead man.

When a woman comes for a reading with a tiny baby's cunt my mom always finds a "Jealous-Evil Eye!" within the labyrinthine blood fractals. Not only does my mother reveal what was, is, and will be to woman who need mystic perspectives that they may empower themselves with, but she is also a St. Joan precipitating with a God glistened blade and heavy sense of being into the dripping crimson flesh-walled caves where angels stick and flap. She vanquishes the threat of the "Jealous Evil Eye!" by dampening the coagulated nucleus, which exists as a pupil, of the eye and piercing the dermis directly beneath it with a syringe sucking the clot and the intrinsic, corporeal foundation contaminated under it. Both the nucleus pupil and the yolk beneath the epidermis under it need both be drawn out so to emasculate the primordial eye and engender a Salomi twitching nystagmus somewhere out there in a healthy human skull. Clamps are latched on to the baby cunt's labia attached to three foot light chains (we are quite weak) pulled alternately on each flank by Asma and I while my mom bombards the little cavity with a pre-heated and formidably sized metal rectangle in an elliptical cream whipping motion. No "Jealous Evil Eye!" has survived as of yet.

My mother separates her sour flower existence from her other modes of being. She is upset with me because I do not; I only have one mode of being. She seems to understand. She thinks I have a Bedouin brain immersed in a bespoken hematological appetite. We do look like each other.

2

We have heavy Siberian Black hair, long and wicked. We have Horrid Big eyes because there is something wrong with us. We have Purgatory Grey irises, though my pupils are perennially contracted inherited from my lulled, decaying father. We have the Wandering Arab skin stretched on a brittle body. We have wistful hair above our Suffocated Blue Dry lips implying a smear of dirt. We have an arch shoving our lower back forward saying we are offering our little belly or our little butt but I think we are not. We have the Mongolian Purple aureoles besieging the Sudanese Purple nipples surmounting boyish bumps. Her cunt is concave, mine convex; hers suggests entry, mine irritation. Our mouth is wide and queer and lurid. I have one fang among my upper teeth. It is on the left. I tease it with my tongue. Our face is religiously pretty though the whole theme synthesized with our body exalts us to a thing profane. Asma looks quite perverse and different.

3

I went to the Masjid to touch flowers. I grazed the soft petals softly with the dirty, gentle fingertips of my left hand because my right is heavy and violent. I floated along the temple's perimeter petting the colors on the colorless green stems with my head tilted flowerwise, sullen face and all. Petals have no temperature; I cannot recall touching stems, for why would I, so the thermometric possibilities they might contain are willfully obscured. I would never be as lewd enough to caress the stigma. The zephyrs are gravid with the floral perfumes of deaths which are really too much for the morning. Flowers have the wrong smell although I have faith they will evolve properly. Before going into the reading house behind the garden at home I will witness their rosy influence and all they have to inherently offer, but when I come out with the brilliant catatonic scents of the room clinging to my wispy moustache I see what they *could* offer. What they could do with their looks and that smell. They are a bit obscene as they are now but wandering here to touch them feels like meaning.

The Imam will not let me on the rugs inside unless I perform Ghusl (sacred bathing). The Masjid's hemispherical facade is bubbling and screaming under the Eastern ubiquitous sickness of the Eastern born sun. The Muezzin is feigning sobriety to it because he thinks it more pious to do as he calls the Idhan for Zuhr Salah. The steadfast advance toward the spigots to make ablution with accustomed but eager countenances. It is something if you think about it really, nothing if you do not. I can actually feel my dirt when I come here and then I think I want it off me.

Ago sometime I used to make salat on the Masjid's rugs in a scrubbed body and a dainty, hinting yellow caftan rife with cerise vines traveling here and there about my figure. Quite choice, really. There stood I kneeling and prostrating with the laity in the round gaping vastness of the room bound by wall inscribed and audibly uttered, infallible revelations. Those words do bind. Often I would try to incite my body to anomalously shake, spin, smack, jump and kick people, but at the utterance of the versicles I would be gravitated with the horde. Qiyam: "Allah-hu-Akbar"-- relentlessly fixed in standing position, still, stillborn; "Allah-hu Akbar"-- back shoved down to form right angle with hands on knees and -- "Sami-la-limon -Hamidah" yanking us upright; Sajdah: "Allah-hu Akbar"-- pulled from the depths of deep with joints hooked to strings despotically shaping our demanded prostration, stringy neck gripped and held making forehead flush with complicit rug. The Prophet (may peace and blessings be upon him) said that the Sajdah position is the closest one can be to Allah in this fleshy life. I suppose for girls like me, too. The Imam must be trying to teach us asceticism because the rugs are so pretty and involute with shapes, colors, lines -- big/little, bright/dim, thick/thin -- yet we are not to think about them whilst among them. It would be a great deal easier to concentrate if we were in a square, flat colored room with flat colored rugs, I think. I do not think this system of me as marionette was in concert with my body on certain days. Eventually it revolted without my decided intent.

Heat is big fingers groping as it always is to one attempting propriety and cleanliness. Nevertheless, the Masjid gets swollen with a sweat dripping, believing throng. Jumma' always draws the reluctant and hesitant in loyalty among the fringes of Allah's comrades. Possibly it is the centripetal rugs with all their wretched lines. I wore my white linen robe embossed with pig pink daisies. I was powerful. I could tramplestomp on Ogre's head. We were in standing position when the Imam began to recite Surat-al-Iqrah -- "... created you from a clot;" I took the reins of my thoughts and began to wonder about bleeding on the rugs. Little drops, I was thinking about.

Then he recited Surat-al-Qariaa':

The Calamity,

what is the Calamity,

what will convey unto thee what the Calamity is;

a day wherein mankind will be as

thickly scattered moths,

and the mountains will become as

carded wool;

then, for those whose scales are heavy

with good works,

he will live a pleasant life;

but for those whose scales are light,

the bereft and hungry one will be

his mother;

what will convey unto thee what she

is --

Raging Fire!

My pelvis was aflutter; Arabic beautifully recited by stern

men as a backdrop to whimsical thoughts can do something to tiny girls. I suppose it can make them young ladies.

No more visions of dripping. Now seen was immanent operas of thick red cascades blanketing the intricacies of the finely embroidered rug. "Allah-hu-Akbar." I put my hands on my knees and I was aware of my crotch. Viscid weight supplanted the sweat-damp region on the lower part of my garment. "Sami-la-limon-Hamida"-- in Qiyam position standing and gushing my rebellion on powerless rug. "Allah-hu-Akbar"-- in Sajdah prostrating and my gory pisser was flush with robe fabric, labia latching onto it for plug but not without imprinting a blood rorschach congealing lower hind to cloth. When we were standing again I could hear a girl about my age whispering, gasping to a young woman -- "shu hadha? Astighfur-Al-lah!" I immediately thought about how Imam Ali (peace be upon him) said no one should say "Astighfur-Al-lah" about another's mishap. The whispering revolt became pandemic amongst the phalanx of girls and women. Sure enough, I was gushing much on the rug, and concurrently quite adamant regarding finishing prayer. I guess the others were too, seeing that they continued murmuring with sacrilegious cephalic twists, for you cannot alter your linear direction of focus in prayer, and willfully going through the prescribed motions. After prayer I looked about myself and area and scurried home propelled by bulbous feminine eyes eating me and lowered to the ground masculine negated gazes vomiting me. When I got home I went expressly to our bedroom, Asma's and mine, took off my garment and flattened it with its seat upward on my bed, and there and then saw a symmetrically stained print of a butterfly or moth with its pretty wings, little big eyes and all. As I stood picking out the quaint details on the wings and committing it to memory lest somebody forces me to clean it, my mother yelled, "Elib, is that you? Ta'al Habibti...come make your mom food. I am too hungry and hot for move."

I walked to the kitchen sticky and naked and did as such.

4

These days and usually every Friday I lope about the house of God with a complacent countenance that peasant peoples perceive as despondent. I would not care if it was not for these sanctimonious strangers asking me "what is wrong?" as they simultaneously are thinking "oh dirty little girl, sad and miserable, I can make you clean and happy." I simper and expose the grandeur of my eyes which sends them a rapidly flashing montage of a hermetic universe interposed with spiraling torsos dangling from ceiling planes opalescent; I instill the size of galaxies and superclusters of galaxies filled with the impeding black matter and gasses hostile to their weak human babies. Then they bound to the rugs of the Masjid with the celerity of fly to flight when sensing she will be touched. Not that I claim this forced vision is the truth but it is just that they should mind their bloody business.

When I catch sight of the Imam or he catches sight of me the trajectory of our eyes vies with one another in speed to evade. His, out of an acceptance that there is an innate pathology within me that if suppressed encourages the pathogens. My elusiveness is merely out of anticipating his estrangement; I do not want to stifle the safe space we tolerate so to compel him to have faith in the hapless task of inducing comfortability between me and objects like himself. I am already too naked. It is a problem. Too naked for all's sense of propriety. And the Imam knows it. He does not think it right or wrong , he just cannot think it within the connotative empire he has to admonish and reproach. I suppose it would be nice to chat. If it was not for coming here I would not sense myself as the emetic bundle of obscenity; I would just feel the wee gauche that I am. I will come, though. If I stop, and sometime future must come back it will be even more awkward. From which, may transgress the comfortable discomfort now living and bring us to a place where others curl and wilt while the Imam stands aloof in his schismatic robes thriving on fleshy horror. I can wait to travel to that place.

The day after blood on the rugs the Imam sent pious sister Fatima to the house. She found me in my sleeping slip and striped socks behind the house. I was digging a hole with my hand amongst bugs jumping and birds lilting , as morning often portends. She was maudlin at the idyllic scene before her meek disposition. Her tight face tightened by strings connected to her pores under her skin attached to spools at her nasal cavities being wound by something otherly. The string must have broke and unwound at a rate proportionate to the tension it borne. Her mouth loosened , cheeks jiggled and eyes doused the whole damn face. There must have been a dam breached as well when the face was released.

"Fatima?" asks a concerned I. Not even a mere grunt was uttered under her twittering lips. I put out my hands, upturned my palms with ear tilted to shoulder miming -- "what is the matter dear old lady?" She gave me a gesture of the hand which I took to say "scoot away, go on now," but which actually meant -- "go on doing the marvelous thing you were doing." If I had taken attention of her endearing smile I may have understood initially. So when I thought "scoot", out of reverence and a need for direction in this frigid warmth I began to walk away toward the postern. With a disheveled leap she grasped my bony shoulders and ushered me back to where I dug. I looked at her vacantly. After I was convincingly seated she put out her palms toward me and gave a shoving motion to the space between us meaning "Halt! Right there; perfecto!" She then walked backwards with eyes gaping at me and hands placing me in a box. She did the "scoot/continue" gesture again so I ignored her and started digging and clawing at the soil. She started slapping her thigh happy and assumed diverse positions descrying me from rare angles. She was not bothering me so I did not bother her.

Nowadays, she speaks little. And she seems to really like me in a peasant to master manner. She is not the pious sister Fatima anymore; she is just the Fatima old woman who talks little because of dirty Elib. The Imam does not blame me but silently implies that I am an unconscious culprit or vessel through which nasty things funnel. He definitely may be right.

I think she is better in this way, nasty as things may seem to the Imam and his many ears who see her as a damned victim and me as a thoughtless reagent. I will dig holes for them.

5

Laying on my too big bed, I started reading a book in a language I like but do not know about orchids. Looking at the pictures I decided they are gorgeously vulgar. A thing I may be. With their scooping lips and orderly random petals deceiving all the little unsuspecting bugs to fly about and breed for them. Possibly the bugs know and they are just nice like that. Or maybe they do not care and have not much else to do at that moment. Maybe it feels just as good as bug to bug hump. Stupid bugs. Asma blankly staring at the mirror brushing her blank hair. That girl is something to fear but I am not afraid of her. I probably love everything or do not know what not liking is. I am positive I could dart over to Asma right now and kiss her much on her dead, wet lips. Yanking her head back by her brushed hair. I do touch her when I am agitated with love for her and I slip into her bed because she is my sister and I love her. She will mutter with cheek pressed to edge of bed. I hope she is thinking of me or a thing like me.

"What do you think of orchids? Do you think them gorgeous?" "Orchids? The flower, Elib?" "Yes, orchids, flowers, more than flowers." "Let me see." I show her pictures of a few that if I were a bug I would definitely hump even if I knew they were orchids. "They're nice, I don't know why you say 'gorgeous', but they are nice flowers." "How about not as flowers? How about as animals, people, or parts of people? What if you looked down your panties and saw one of those?"-- I, pointing to a voluptuous specimen. " Mmm, it is hard to say, Elib... maybe it would be nice in my hair; what if you saw what is 'down your panties' sitting on a stem where an orchid sits?"-- she flicks my cunt like a drunk old penis beast putting on a show for his mates, all chortling and me bashfully blushing with slave contempt. "Ouch, do not do that Asma! What if I hit you there?" "I would bind you to your huge 'gorgeous' bed with rough 'gorgeous' ropes and let the mangy dogs lick you with their dirty tongues all over your orchid drenching your smelly petals and crumpling them all up!" "No you would not!," says I.

Even if she did let that happen to me I believe she would feel bad afterward and do something to make me feel better; somehow. She probably does not believe that she would. I lay on my bed and she on hers. "If you are upset with me, then here, hit mine... as hard as you wish," says she. " I do not want to hit yours Asma, just please do not do it again." "Yes, Elib, yes; if it is what you wish." Odd where she gets the impetus to speak from, for I know her mind is listless and body impressionably supple, susceptible to its molder.

While turning the lamp around toward the wall so Asma could sleep I was flooded with sadness when I espied a still ladybug on the lip of the casing under the scalding bulb's heat. Death, death, death, oh lord, such a death! Asma would feign concern for my sake but it would end up being more harmful to the dead ladybug if the girl was roused. Its wings took on an albino tint, unless it was a living albino, and they were spread in wanting flight. Surely the heat could not have been as powerful as to torch it to death or immobility before it could flee.

No, that is not what happened. Possibly, it died of old age and its body was mutilated by the heat after it died; wings spread as an "I was a ladybug once" gesture. If it was living, in good health, and it wanted to flee when sensing the glass bulb's death rays it could have just flapped its spotted wings and found refuge in some cool, healthy crevice. Perhaps it was tired of having to flap and leave cozy little niches every moment a despot decides it wants a little light or some fire to make its mother dinner. Perhaps it was challenging its forced, choiceless biology it was given. It said to the bulb -- " I do not have to leave at the advent of your incident glory... I will hang about a little longer than usual, then leave." And its wings became crisp, flimsy legs brittle. Maybe it was just sick of the beetle way.

"Go ahead light, burn me and my adorable tinyness to pointless ashes!" "Alas! I am alone in this too tight universe amongst poor roaches and monomaniac ants. Rarely do I encounter other strays of my own kind... and if I do, they treat me as a foreigner with their freshly pollinated bodies shunning my domicile dusty thorax. Then they leave, and I stay. What could I possibly do out there with them? Yes, this is wretched, but this is the wretched I bear because I am aware of the hostile vastness that is wrought when one leaves their allowed place. Those other beetles are not jolly, they are just comfortable. At least I am truly miserable. Even if I tried to assimilate back into the dewy stalks and soft piles on magnetic flowers I would still be aware of this place, hence -- cringing from the otherness intruding.

So this light that burns so bright, burns too bright to see."

"Hot! Hot! AAAGHH! Ouch! It is hot! It burns!" That tragedy is tragic indeed.

I must do something with this fastly frying integument. I could incinerate it properly seeing that that may have been its intentions initially. It seems a little too queer to bury any-thing. I will eat it and say "Bismi-Lahir-Rahmanir-Raheem" for it and it will be the good thing for it. While trying to get it out of the lamp I under-gauge my monstrous hand and send it diving under the bed. I cannot remove it without making a clatter and waking my nothing sister whom I do not want to bother; I will continue tomorrow. It may be nice for it to just decay under the bed or possibly feed its peasant, but friendly neighboring ants. "Bismi-Lahir-Rahmanir-Raheem."

6

I love God often. In his coy wrath and mercy. If I clearly envisage the Prophet (may peace and blessings be upon him) I cry. And his grandson Husayn (peace be unto him) with his foreseen, willful tragedy at Kerbala. One by one they advanced toward that whorish army and conquered them by dying, as the weak baby gains sympathy by inviting the incubus to violate its softness and make it pule. Yes, Husayn (peace be unto him) wins with his head in the enemy's hands uplifted. His eyes still supplicating the sole war determinant in the ether to proceed with what must occur next. And Ali ibn Abu Talib, (peace be unto him) Husayn's father wed to the Sacred Daughter of the Prophet, being decapitated in Koofa while praying. Such a kafiruun shall expect the tortures of something otherly that I cannot say but take delight in knowing it will happen. Who is better in punishment than He who compels the toady angels to rip half of the face off alternately with hooks while the other side heals? That is really nothing, though, just language. We can do much. If we must. Bloody, the deaths of the House of the Prophet. The pool of Abundance in the Jannah incarnadined by them spurred by my and their pretty Allah.

A tinier girl than my present smallness I stretched on the bed my playful, scabby limbs.

I implored this god for a micro act for a micro girl. A very fair request if one knows what fair is. Or cares. There and then heavy epileptic jolts shook those limbs. A superfluous answer for a tiny query and a puny girl, I might say. I will say. Did He not consider how fragile I was and how huge I know He must be?

7

Laylia's palest black skin suggested my cunt slide the whole area of the clit she owns.

It feels so wonderful and isolated to be wanted for touch. I sat on the friendly bench next to the postern every recreational period eating my fruit and drinking my milk. But because of the demanded fast in Ramadhan, I just sat and made my eyes appear as if they were looking at the negative space between girls playing rather than the girls themselves. Difficult with them skipping and leaping all about like hyper particles.

Laylia intruded my space watching with her suspiciously non-intrusive heat. "I am sitting here because a boy last night was hellishly loud. I live with uttering, with that froggish hellishness eating my torturous mind. You have to go to reading class next, yes?" "I thought we all have to go?"-- I, assuming normal voice. "Yes we all must go but I am bleeding now so I cannot read so I sit in back and bleed and watch and think wretched"--she, joyous with down crestfallen eye at last words. "Oh, so you do not have to make Salat or any such thing as that?" "No nothing with that glorious joy as if bitter jinns were flooding out of me huh? Ha ha they're dumb. You bled?" My mouth has nothing to say, but do not worry, I am not frightened. She fills a gap that is only a gap because of her -- "you have those big huge pathetic eyes so beautiful I want them. Wow, with your hair out. That would be something I want." I would have loved to give her some eyes then and there; I do not want to have a thing somebody else wants. It saddens me wholly. I let her know what I want from her. "My sister Asma has bled some I think, and my mom bleeds, and some other people I have seen. I enjoy watching your skin, I have watched it before but never this close. I would like to see where it is that skin is made like yours."

"It is different than yours -- here." She grabbed my wrist and placed the face of my stupid hand against her different cheek. Hot cheek, punishable, magnetic wet, needy. She released my wrist and as a sad, lorn ladybug said, "please look at the pretty I am, you can have me, just don't stomp on me. You must take me lest I get stomped." My fingers heard the ladybug and are not as rude as to stop grazing her cheek from mouth corner to Hijab edge. The veiled sisters were thieving glances out of their naked obvious eyes. Of course, in their veiled huddle apart. Laylia saw my concern and killed the sad ladybug by turning her head, imparting the sacrilegious girl's face to them forcing their eyes to the trampled dirt. I knew her mastery over lowly me and the veiled sisters.

"They shouldn't look at anything save thick black cloth those damned harlot nasties.

Do you talk to them? You should not, it is not a good thing to do" says Laylia.

"Nobody talks to me, even veiled sisters. I am so disgusting, Laylia. I am horrible, Laylia. I am horrible, Laylia. I am horrible, Laylia. I am telling you the most important thing ever." My cunt is dying with the twirling swirliness of flat repetition.

"Why are they wearing those veils, Laylia? Why are they wearing those veils, Laylia."

"Because they are alive and ugly, little beast."

I have seen one of the veiled girls unveiled in the wash-room. She was sickeningly beautiful. Laylia is not a liar, though. Laylia asked me if I would join her for some time when school-time ended. I said I would.

Before playtime ceased, Laylia requested that I go with her to the bathroom. There, she extracted a tubular blood-soaked cloth from her cunt and placed it on a window-sill where no window occurs. She handed me a fresh roll of gauze and ordered me to wind it into a cylinder, tightly. I started doing what she wanted of me. She was bestriding the toilet, raising her skirt and shoving some mature mauve panties down over her sparkling stockings and scooping water from toilet onto ruddy slit.

CANTO 3

SHADOW
THINGS

14

TreeGirl

William approached the field where the girl, or a semblance to a girl, exists. He does not know how to reconcile what he is seeing but he cannot disturb his journey by hindering its movement for the sake of fear. She, her jaundiced skin is reverberating in the harsh light. The field and tree in respect to placement appear a bit queer here. But the girl. How can this be?

" Girl? Girl? What would you like? I have some water...food...things, things you may have never known!" William does not know if this girl can even hear him. William touches her flesh and she jumps, slamming her head against the tree trunk.

Before William's eyes is a tree in the middle of a dirt field with nothing else seeming different than the dirt for as far as possibly visible. Around this tree's trunk is a girl's arms grafted to each other at the wrist, with the girl filthy and nude connected to such arms. She is laying her head with ear to bark against tree. William does not know where he is but he does find himself aroused which is disturbing him because it would be quite easy to go inside of this girl. At least, that is how it seems.

William turned his head for a moment and when he returned it he saw a short little man approaching the girl with a very worker sort of demeanor about his presence.

" Sir, may I ask you where we are and who this girl is, and what is the reason for her condition?"

"Naa," replied the worker.

This worker walked right up to the buttocks of the girl and began to shove a phallus in the girl's cunt and then in her ass. This continued until the girl seemed as if she was not moving with it anymore. The worker stroked the girl's hair in a somewhat daughterly manner, and then left to where he came from. William was shocked at what he had just seen. Watching what was happening to her found its way of arousing William and he now thought that maybe the girl wants him to do as such. He thought that if she were not so dirty, in addition to discolored skin, she would be quite attractive. What was he thinking about, though, at a time like this? He doesn't know where he is and how he came to be in this place.

Once again, he approached the girl and this time he began to rub her head. She began to smile and murmur. He could not help but have the strongest erotic attraction for this girl; he did not want her clean, actually, he liked her even bound as she was. But what can she really do if he just...he decided he would try to talk with her once more.

" What is your name?" Asked William.

To this she continued to smile as he stroked her. She must have been placed here by someone, though. Surely, this is not her nature. These are themes that William thought as he stroked her hair now. He noticed that he was close enough that his erection was actually touching her through his pants on her rib cage. She had quite the mane. It was in clumps at places but because of how greasy it was it managed to not dreadlock. He began to move his erection around her, just grazing her in order to see what her reaction would be.

He decided that this is a thing that she surely wanted, especially after witnessing the phallus scene and all. He got behind her and lowered his pants and began to try to go inside her when she started making a hyena sort of sound as she banged her connected wrist against the tree and tried to turn her head to look at him. He stopped immediately and got in front of her in order to find out what was wrong, if she was hurt or something. She just cocked her head to the side looking at him with pleading eyes and then looking to her wrists and then signaling to his wrists. He knew what she wanted now, she wanted to be rid of this damn confinement. He did not blame her, how could any body endure such a thing. He looked around frantically and as if by magic, he found an old chisel, and an old saw right next to each other. He decided that the saw would be far too powerful for her tiny wrists and might cause too much bleeding. He decided to go with the chisel instead.

After chiseling away for some time he began to really become attached to this girl as she moaned and grinded her teeth in fits of unimaginable pain, so it was decided, she would come with him and be rid of this land. She did bleed quite a bit but eventually she was freed, and she still bled as he got to finally satisfy this lust for her. When the morning arrived, she lay dead and naked, next to William, who was alive and naked. She bled to death during the night. The cloth that they used was not good enough because as he looked closer at her now separated wrists, he saw that there were nerves and veins that were once connected that he cut. He happened to turn his head as he began to weep and saw the worker man approach, the same one from the day before. William just put his head in his hands, rocking himself in discomfort. The worker man said he had just come back for his tools that he left. William, shocked that the worker did not even make a comment about the girl, just kind of pointed him to the general direction of the saw and the bloody chisel. The worker man did say one more thing, though.

"Hey, sir ? How come you ain't just use the tree saw to cut down the tree?"

15

Lilian John

I am more so than not - a quiet pretty girl. The thing and things that I do, only for some few years, demands that I must know a group of solely men, as different from each other as fingers from windows, but are not discussed due to the ugliness associated with the glue that binds them - I talk of johns, men who supplant their money with warm mouths, moist eyes, and hands that listen. Of course, I have spoken with plenty, but all under the umbrella of work, and they tell me so many things, everything you need to know really, and if I told it all, that good person listening to me would know the nausea, the nausea of the soul from hearing the same human conditions in all these men, an also themselves. So I shrug my shoulders back and drop to the poor pleading floor these other men's hollow, but too heavy stories, that still yap as accents and dialects spread in all directions flat over the town ground, and more than just the weight, I discarded those stories of johns so that I may find even just some key words to tell you in the tale of Lillian, who was also a john, and the most softest whispering fragile man I have touched and stared at. Of the other clients, I know more than their wives, pets, or mothers they still live with; of Lillian, it is really quite a shame that there is as much known about him as there is God. There is nothing. There is nothing out there telling a thing about this tiptoeing man. This is a loss to the study of everything because *he* was the exception to everything. Nothing can be positively said about this boyish john who blinks coyly with his butterfly wing eyelashes as half of his pale long body is still behind the door trying to rationalize his paranoia to face the next room. Only things revealed about him from documents with real professional stampings and letter headings should be considered. I will tell the wondrous delights of what I have known of this barely in existence creature from the first time that he sent a note to me saying that he may possibly be interested in finding out if he would like to discuss things with a girl as pretty as he thinks I may be sometimes. Oh, yes, and there is another thing about him, but, well, we will see about that later.

Firstly, before I tell you of the first touch between the dainty pink lipped john and I, it would be rude of me if I failed to give you a very faint impression of myself, what a thing as I does, and possibly even - where; this is really for the reason of giving the audience a more vivid image/scene of the goings on between the person we all want to really hear of, and I, which I will tell when all that is needed for a successful telling has been fulfilled. Oh, well, this really is embarrassing, I am so shy, you know. Okay, well, I lived in the big city when I was really quite a small girl, at an age that it was indecent to even think about me the way that all do now; youth has that protection, even if they are thinking it, no? It was in a neighborhood surrounded by many neighborhoods that had immigrants, freed slaves, just darker than our little streets. The people were darker, the buildings, the clothes, the pavement, even the sun didn't waste much of its energy over around there. My father did not like any of those people. I think my dad was afraid that the darkness was edging in on our neighborhoods so he moved us out onto a house on an open field in the smallest of places, but still only a couple hours travel to the city. I would have rather had the darkness in our old neighborhood than the wide open field that refuses to give a place to hide from the sun that I never asked for anyway. It was boring out there, and nobody liked me, so I started fucking boys to make friends with them. I would fuck lots of things, even had a friend for a long time in a guy who was a business partner with my dad in building things. This work is really not that bad. At first, in the beginning I was doing anal but realized quite late that men have an obsession with wedging in huge objects into tiny holes; I mean it is like they want to rip something apart. And not all johns have the tiniest of cocks. Most do, but then you will get some short quiet white man who is balding and cannot look at you in the eyes when you first open the door for him, but in ten minutes is trying to stuff this huge dick in your ass. I cannot say anything at that point because I have to be fair; what am I going to say, "You can fuck my ass if you have an erect cock under 4 inches?" The real spoiler for all the other ass-fuck lovers is when this Paul guy brought a pretty healthy-sized dildo over and put it in my ass. Next week, he does the same, which is strange because he gave me the last one that was brand new in the package, and now he brings another new one, but this time it hurts more. I do not know if it is just me or what. Oh yeah, also, this guy has on all these rubber gloves and baby wipes when he comes over wiping me and him at almost every touch. That is not the way to flatter a girl. Anyway, when he leaves he leaves the dildo again, and I put it next to the other one and notice that it is a bit bigger. I am starting to think about changing my policy. I know a lot of girls who do well who don't get buggered. Well, here we go again, he does it again, but with a huge one, and afterward he makes me gag on his cock to the point where I vomited. He was laughing at me. I only gagged because he was shoving my face down. He could tell that I couldn't deep throat it. He was laughing as I was puking on his cock, physically suffering, you know. He ruined it for everybody and now I do not do anal with anybody except my fiance. I mean, I like anal sex, but not with straight cocks, only with ones that curve up. I only masturbate in my butt, but not with monstrous-sized things, just my finger.

16

Le Princesse Fasciste

All of these creatures, little and big, shrank at her. They would know better than to run too fast if they even had the notion of her possibly watching them. On occasion, she would pet and convince one of the creatures that she really loved them; this was short-lived, though, because whenever one wanted some time alone, or away from her, she would take it as a lack of manners and punish the creature. Her punishments were of many kinds; she twist their skin so that their eyes bulged out, put her mouth on their nose and blew as hard as her too-healthy lungs let her, and most often, more for her own erotic fulfillment than for the sake of even satisfying her sadistic needs, she would manipulate the genitalia of the poor things.

The princess, le princess fascist, would give speeches every day exclaiming her great love for all of her pets. She really felt that she loved them at times, but she could not help herself from wanting so much control over them that she wanted them to understand that there is the possibility of her waking up in the middle of the night and making one of them pee into another one's mouth. She did want them to feel love, but love the abuse, love it because it is the only closeness they will experience in their little miserable lives. At times she would question her own self and want to stop what she was doing, once even she let one go free after she twisted its genitals so bad that it started to bleed from the mouth. It would not stop whimpering, and she does not like to see any physical effects of great harm that she inflicts on them, she just wants to know that they are suffering when she wants them to suffer, which is often. The one she set free came back anyway because it was too scared and did become attached to the abuse; that is what she believes. She made it feel welcome for a little while, nestled it in her arm, and then went into such a rage that all began to whimper. She actually bit off the little scared creatures balls and shoved them in its mouth while swinging its head against the wall which all suffer within.

She writes to God about her speeches every night before going to bed and after praying to her God. Here is an excerpt from one of these nights:

2/12

They need me, I don't need them, but it is my duty to take care of them and teach them because who else will if I don't?

Oh, lord, will you let them understand that I do what I do for their own good? Look what you do for our own good, I am trying to be just like you because they say you are the best example for mankind, and even though I am a woman, that is a kind of man, mama said that, at least. I do know that tomorrow I will tell them that they will have to learn how to get rid of all their own poop some how without me having to always clean it up because I don't always make them clean my poo, right, Lord God? And ever since little Bessie broke all her teeth she's been looking at me all funny and strange like she's going to try and do something. Lord, I hope she ain't that dumb, because I will whoop her something right! You know what I am saying, Lord? Tomorrow I am going to tell them that they should feel privileged to even have someone like me to be close to them, however that closeness is. Love ain't always sweet, is it Lord? Well, I am going to go to bed, well, after I check on them so that they don't think that I ain't trying to watch them when they think they all alone and stuff. I love you Lord God, and I want you to love me, too.

"We have to get out of here before she gets us all, Bessie. We know that you know the way out through the house, don't you?" Igor the penguin asked.

" It down't mattow... sshee gon sswee everything!" Replied a toothless Bessie.

" Yes, of course it matters, look what she did to you! Look what she did to Herbert! Do you want that to happen to all of ..."

" What are we all talking about? Huh? Well, I will deal with you later. Right now I must deliver maybe one of my best speeches yet," says the princess.

The princess climbs onto a sort of makeshift platform with a sort of stand in this concrete backyard of hers encased by a wall ten feet high. She twirls her curls as everybody rushes to their respective spots. She darts a vicious look toward Bessie, and then scans the whole room with that same vicious look. She quickly changes her countenance into a pleasant innocent little girl that the rest of the world assumes her to be. She clears her wicked throat and commences to shout.

" Pets! Pets! Pets! Today is a new day in the Kingdom and Queendom of Me. I shall no longer be lowered to the depths to dirty my royal hands with the poop of your butts. You will find a way to dispose of it as promptly as it is expelled from the body. I do not care how this task is accomplished, just get it done! I know what you all think... yes, I know that you think that I am a bit hard and that maybe I over punish you guys. If this is what you really think, then I dare you as I dared Herbert to go. Remember what Herbert did? He came back! We do not accept failures here. If you think you can make it, go ahead, prepare a list of who wants to leave and I will grant it. That is all for this day of our Queen, Me."

All the creatures are confused. If this is true, where will

they go? As they are pondering this, Igor looks up into the alley sky and sees a huge billboard saying:

" How would you like free housing, an education, a career, a purpose?"

Igor showed everybody the sign and they replied to it saying " me, me, me, me!" It continued to conclude as:

"Be a soldier in the war on terror, now!"

All the creatures were riled up and had one idea pumping through their mind.

Bessie spoke up and said, " ist twime to kwick thwat cwunt's cwunt intwo hew mowf!"

" YEEAAAHH!" is how all the creatures responded.

As soon as the princess heard all this commotion she came out to the concrete encasing and demanded to know what was going on right this instant. So, instead of telling her, they showed her.

17

Bone Jumping

" . . .that lady, the one with the three sons who all had that greasy hair and all . . .and all three of them fagged out of the army . . .Mrs. Eleanor, or Ms. Eleanor, whatever . . .I am quite positive that she is completely a dead-rotting-hag lady as we speak . . .positively!," little, tiny Elizabeth insisted as she continued to jump on the back of some corpse. The corpse seemed to belong to a very developed woman, as did the cold house they were in seem to belong once to a developed family, but that must have been quite a time ago as the house reveals with its rotting wood and dry dust harmonizing with damp breaths of hallway passages.

As a mouse speaking to a rat, Charlie replied with, " I suppose you may be right . . .it's just that..." It was hard for Charlie to talk sometimes when Elizabeth was jumping, not because of what she was jumping on, for she jumps on many things, but because he could see her little bump in her panties, and he could only enjoy it because she wasn't conscious of him looking.

"Just that what? C'mon, spit it out!"

"It's just that I think I would have heard of it because one of those boys that left the service used to work at the shops with one of my cousins on my mom's side...but I don't even like my mom's side, there all a bunch of queers...but if that lady was alive right there, do you think she would die by you jumpin' on her back as such?," Charlie asked. Charlie did not have a problem with corpse jumping, but he liked watching Elizabeth do it instead.

"Are you finished yet? That is why you are not sure? Because some fucking homo related to your mum hasn't said a word of it, yet?! Well...," says Elizabeth.

"I don't think...I don't believe they're all ho..."

"Oh, you said it yourself. Shut up. And no, I do not think she would die by me just doing this," Elizabeth says as she slows down her pace of jumping on the body.

"...homo," says Charlie, confusedly.

"What?"

"Homo. Oh, I was just finishing what I wa..."

"But...," Elizabeth gets a gleam in her eye as if she just realized a very important thing as she steps off the big chested body's back and gets in front of its head, "...if I did this!" Elizabeth winds her leg back and kicks the woman's head, letting her shiny black shoe's mirror buckle shove into the nose. "And this, and this!" Elizabeth repeats with each kick.

"That *would* do it," small Charlie remarks.

"I think so!," Elizabeth exclaims.

"It really would," says Charlie.

" Sure the fuck would!," yells Elizabeth.

" I would do it, too, but I can't get all that dead people stuff all over my clothes and shoes...I'd get beat quite hard for that one." Charlie may regret that or may be relieved by it as he is looking down at his ragged, stained clothes. Stains from history's happenings, not dirty, not smelly.

" It is not as if your clothes are that nice or anything. Look at my clothes, not a spot...and my clothes are a hundred times better than yours."

Those words made him pause in character. He stood as a brooding man for quite a time trying to find his way back to the current moment through the innocent imagery of harsh memory. He must have found his way back to the present before he revealed so, giving him time to decide how to attack the little bad mouthed Elizabeth. Rashly, he decided to mirror her spite when he blindly fired the following.

" Ah, so you think you're better than I, little miss Worthington?... If my family kissed the royal ass we might have nice clothes, too...even though my father works for yours, he could probably squeeze HIS FUCKING EYEBALLS OUT... FOREVER! ...Still, you're ugly, even with your nice clothes!" Charlie turns away from Elizabeth suggesting that he is doing something that he does not want her to see. It is not as if he has a severe problem with the rich, but it is just that he is tired of having to feel bad and lower because of a stupid little thing like money.

Elizabeth looks at him for a moment with concern and then quickly dismisses it just to re-assume her face of not caring about anything.

" Quit being a baby...are you crying? Ah, whatever. If you

really wanted to do it you would... you never do it. You never touch them. Because of your clothes? I definitely do not think so! Maybe *you* are the queer one, Charlie. Are you? A bit, or a lot, queer, Charlie? Can you not touch a woman? Even a stanky, rotting one?"

" I can do whatever I like! And I am not no fairy gay man!," says Charlie as he spins around to face her. It appears as if his eyes are a little reddened.

" 'Not no?' That means you are queer, Charlie."

" You know I am not. I touch Jen Rottenberger almost every week at bible class... she..."

" Rot-ten-ber-ger? She is a Jewess, yes? Must be with that name. I do not think that counts, Charlie. You got anything else?"

" She ain't no Jew...Jewess...if she is, she's a girl just as you!"

" And how do you know that I am a girl? You never seen anything. Since we first met at the company party you have always thought me to be a boy, huh?" Elizabeth boyishly states this last remark with a tone of suggestion. She is sitting on the dead woman's stomach now, the corpse having been flipped over from all the kicking. Elizabeth is slowly spreading her legs by separating her knees and revealing the undergarments of the upper class. Charlie turns around abruptly.

"' Lizabeth, what are you doing? Quit playin' round so much."

" Oh, I love it when you say my name, Charlie. Please do it again. Actually, could you come over here and help me out for a moment?" Elizabeth, now assuming a huskier sort of voice, says.

" What? Help you with what? You don't need no help. You're just messing with me like always."

" No, Charlie! How could you say as such? Look, I will give you five pounds if you come over here and help me."

" You ain't got no five pounds...let me see it."

Elizabeth pulls out the money and waves it around like a treat for a dog. Charlie turns around and sees it in addition to her skirt hiked all the way up and her knees all the way spread. He turns back around and takes a deep breath. He faces her and is looking at her face trying to concentrate so that he does not look down at her bare panties and begins to walk toward her. He gets to right in front of her and tries to grab the money.

" No, no, no...not yet. Let me see your hand."

" Why?"

" Let me see your hand?"

Charlie begrudgingly gives her his hand and turns his head to the side, shaking it, pretending to be in disbelief, and not enjoying it. She quickly grabs his hand and just as he looks down she puts it down under her panties. She then leaves his hand there and lets go of it and leans back a bit, smiling. Charlie looks at his hand but does not move it.

" There is your money," says Elizabeth, complacently smiling, motioning to the crotch of the dead woman.

18

Aminah's Hair and Idris' Head

I

Something occurred in Baghdad. There is a boy that is definitely little and small with a head that is quite big but pretty with thick black hair streaming in two different angles toward the horizon behind him. He is not just a little and small boy, though, he is also a member of the Youth Battalion, 2nd division, and quite proud. He, and his commanders, are very sure that he has the ability to spill enemies' blood by the buckets if the reason made itself known. He stood up on his bed rising from the many dreams that were twirling and bouncing in his giant skull moments previous. He looked to the ceiling with confusion and disappointment; he always thought that if he stood on his bed that he would bang and bruise his head on the ceiling's rotting whiteness, not because of his head and wanting to damage the bigness of it, but because his bed was so high. He knew *he* was not higher than the long ruler's tip all the boys in his Battalion could closely gaze down at, his hair was, but his eyes were almost as wide as the damn thing. Just to touch the upper edge he had to climb all the wooden crates (everybody in the neighborhood contributed to this project) by strategically placing his feet and hands in the proper notches, he knew better than to climb with naked feet and hands so as to not impale himself with something as trifling as a splinter.

Whenever coming down from the majestic heights of his bed he would consider hurting his head, and the crumbling ceiling, and keep his head low and back hunched. It really has been a waste of time and energy, all that ducking and hunching. How ridiculous was it that he could stand completely erect and only graze the thinner ends of his straight bristly hair when on tiptoes. At some point expressly after these invisible mumblings and grievances paused to breathe he felt something in between irritation and frustration at the awakening to the knowledge that all this mayhem about him and the ceiling had made him forget almost every detail of his many different dreams. The only thing he could remember was his own self in his own front room spinning that thing that he always plays with but cannot remember, and maybe never actually knew, the name. He knew that some old man, a relation, told him, "man, woman, and children underneath it clinging to their parents in West take shelter from God's punishment with it...but it only is taste...it is not real punishment...it is to let them understand warning before big not understandable to people punishment happen." He just spins it.

But, possibly, he thought, if he recreates that part of the dream other occurrences will attach itself to it as it did in the dream. If he spins the..."babala?," he thought it may be called, then the same things will always happen after the same acts, and the same in dreams, too. He put on his climbing gloves and thick socks, rolled up his sleeping pants, and went to his task.

"Mikhail, where is my baalla?," Idris asks looking up quite high to see his brother's face, or more so his chin.

"It is gone. There is no thing baalla; there is ball. But you do not have a ball, and the only ball you have ever seen is Hassan's last year at the funeral. I know what you want, but you can't say it, so you can't have it...and it is not yours, also." Mikhail does not appear to be playing with his little brother as he moves from right in front of the child toward the door as he would have had this conversation not happened at all. He resolutely opens the door without signs of possibly just assuming a role, the role of not caring whether little Idris gets the unnamed object he expressed to want to locate for most likely a legitimate reason.

"Ooblala? Ooblala!," says Idris, thinking he has named the unnamed. Mikhail stops movement with back still facing the of a sudden excited boy. "Where is ooblala, Mikhail? Mikhail, ooblala, where? Mikhail?," says Idris, desperation touching the petite soldier's last word.

With his back still addressing his younger brother as if this is the accepted manner with which people, everybody, converses with one another, Mikhail replies.

"Your wrong. You are very, very wrong but in some ways closer than the first time. It's probably in one of the closets somewhere, though." Mikhail leaves. Idris' body heaves heavy and sighs too weak to be proportionate to the heave; his arms go a bit limp, just dangling, and his face has the countenance of attempting to decide what countenance to display for such a difficult moment and also to be in harmony with the heave and sigh, which he failed its execution slightly. With Mikhail gone the front room does not seem as bleak with just little Idris standing in it. Possibly because the emptiness is apparent when a teenager such as dissatisfied Mikhail who notices emptiness himself, and the reasons for having a room glutted to the walls with nothing, is in the room. For Idris, anything in the room would just get in the way of the games he plays with his ooblala, like twirling in one spot with it gripped by one hand.

As to make use of this barren room, and so as to resolve his original crisis, Idris looks for his hidden object in the closets. Strangely, this boy's attention does not sway with the various interests one could have with all the other objects he comes across. And they do own a ball. When he emerges from that hole his old, old mother is sitting on the floor near the far wall, and the most possibly away from the window one can be, hunched over sewing on her machine. Idris always wastes time and wanders away in his little body when watching his mother sew with her one arm ending just a bit after an unnecessary elbow and one very calloused hand competing in speed with the machine. The old wooden floor, that can only claim the color of many years and nothing else, does not even shudder at the frantic machine, but the jaundiced walls have nothing to shield it from bouncing the sound back and forth to each other. Quite dark out already, the only light in the room is the small bulb on her intermittently firing machine.

"Mama, where is my...ooblala?"

"I throw it somewhere...I tell your brother throw it somewhere and he take it out when you sleeping...why? Is so dirty...garbage, habibi, play with baala."

"I hate baalaa, I want the baabballa, and I have nothing else and you take it from me...where is it, mama?!" Idris does not like what is happening and is crying but kind of ashamed of it.

"Idris, habibi...please go get water for the dinner...yalla, hurry, I am tired, habibi."

Idris stomped out of the room battling the machine for echoes off the walls but did not slam the door and wouldn't do such a thing because he knew it would break. After the somber effect of gently shutting the door following his raging footsteps he realized that he forgot the bucket inside. When he went back for it he tried to not look at his mother.

"I think maybe your toy will still be by the garbage...if you find it you keep it is okay, but wash hands from jeefa smell, habibi...yalla, fast," says the sewing lady.

Idris thought that he didn't need her to tell him that, he was going to do it anyway, but he probably wouldn't have thought of washing his hands, so it wasn't a waste.

As he kicks the dirt dangling the brown bucket's metal handle from his neck with the bucket proper bouncing on his spine he steps on the stomach of a rotting soldier. This is not so unlikely seeing that Idris takes quite high steps, which would land the bottom of his feet right onto the stomach of about anybody laying, with exception to an extremely obese lady or man; most would have had the uncouth experience of tripping on the corpse. Bringing his other foot onto the stomach and balancing his full body's weight on the once-armed man's tummy Idris takes a moment to stare at the face of his platform. A very queer thing indeed was what he then saw - his sought-after and misnamed umbrella toy's curved handle hooked through the nostril and coming out of the mouth of this guy with everything still perfectly intact; and oddly enough it was standing perfectly up from that nostril with the button pushed in and the red fabric spread tautly over the dead guy protecting him from fake punishment. He would have rather had his umbrella found safe and in a state of solitude, but here it was, glorious as ever, ready to be twirled to reveal last night's mystery, or if not, just to be spun.

He did become aware that his brother was nihilistic enough, and disrespectful of all the Battalion's glorious emblazoned colors, to do such an anarchistic thing as this. He would definitely report him to the correct sirs. He recognized the face as being the brother of a girl who is very known to him, and vaguely known to all the Battalions by way of all her brothers and father being festooned by machine gun markings. He wondered if this was the last brother. This girl, Aminah, was his nanny on the weekends when his mother had to cook for an important religious family in the outskirts; Idris also combed her long beautiful black hair for her after coming back from congregational prayer at the Masjid. She would give him money, and he would smile a smile befitting of a boy as small and pretty as he.

Regardless, he wanted his toy, and he turned the bucket

toward the front protecting his tummy with the handle now putting pressure on the nape of his neck; he became aware that someone may think he was an enemy, seeing that he was still in his sleeping clothes standing over a local dead soldier with his toy rising out of the head like a victorious army's banner, and that considered he thought a patriot like himself would and could yank on the bucket behind him and choke him with the handle.

Having made precautions he went for his umbrella trying to unhook it reversing the path it must have traveled to be hooked in the manner that it was, and even more bothersome was that at the slightest pull the whole head came off with the toy so that when lifting the umbrella up with his hand on the upper handle just above the head, that same head seemed to be staring to the very weird heavens at a bit of a slant, which was nothing more than slippage allowance. He tried to separate the two seemingly non-relative objects. He released the button and tied down the fabric of the umbrella so as to make this less of a spectacle as a task, and as something one may see. He even put his tiny feet astride the now pointy toy standing on the head so it would be anchored, but because he was not able to just pull it up and out because of the way it was hooked, when he tried to pull it out, it resulted as him appearing as if he was on a pogo stick; a rotting head umbrella pogo stick. There Idris was, just hopping on the back of his older comrade's head, and his gorgeous haired nanny's brother's head, but still with both of his clenched fists around his toy.

Idris, tired from his efforts, set the damned connected objects in front of him and stared at it, maybe trying to see if there was a solution that he did not see, or maybe deciding if he could enjoy them as they were, as they possibly were meant to be. He did notice that the mouth seemed to be sucking the curved handle, but in reverse, and how that would feel in one's own throat and mouth also struck him as interesting. He knew he should just get rid of it, even if his umbrella was permanently attached. It wasn't fair, he thought, that is, this God damned place and the stupid things that occur. He finds his toy, and he might have to give it up. He did not want to be accused of this murder, and that girl was so dear to his mother that surely his mother would take sides against him, especially if the girl makes his mother some nice dessert, or something. He looked around, and at least thought he was blessed enough to be close to the garbage site where he would find something to conceal this possible problem. Suddenly, he thought about the last time a traitor was discovered in the ranks, and all that boy did was say that maybe the Battalion was killing too many people before finding out who they were. Something very bad happened to that little boy.

Idris had the end of the Umbrella with the head on it down his stretchy sleeping pants as he walked over to the garbage piles; it appeared as if he had a bulging disease of the right knee. He found some old newspaper with the Leader's face taking up the whole page, and when people see that face their usual reaction is to turn away lest they sneeze, or cough, in the direction of an image of the Leader; Idris just thought-what if somebody accidentally vomited on His face?! So, he decided that that was the best possible thing to conceal it with, save the paper noise.

"Hey, EEE-DREE-SAAA, WHERE AM I, EE-DREEEE-

SA?" Idris knew the masked voice to be that of his possibly criminal brother, and maybe here to bribe him.

"Go away...I will kill you...mom told me she was gonna' kill you anyway, and she hates you because everybody thinks you are stupid and you kiss the boys who kiss boys...so she won't even be mad at me...I will kill you." Idris had some fear in his voice, but not from his brother obviously, but because of the situation. Who would believe his brother over him. But Idris does not really lie; he will have to, he decided. There was silence, but a very heavy silence, the silence of things there who can make sound but are not.

"Aah, Idris, be nice little brother, you always say you are going to kill me but never you do. Oh, I believe you will, but please, Idris, don't do that to me, I'm your friend." Mikhail said this so rife with sarcasm that Idris could feel it. Mikhail added, "Hey, did ya' find that umbrella of yours? Oh, what's that? You have it right there in your hands?" Mikhail was giggling as he finished stating that he knew something, but he still remained out of sight.

Idris, sick of this nonsense, fed right into it and pulled the umbrella out of his pants as if he was unsheathing a sword holding it from the top so that the head was held high, as some sort of battle trophy.

"Oohh, is this what you speak of? Yeah...I found it," and he sheathed the umbrella with head in pants again at the end of his words. His brother came out from behind a garbage pile with eyes gaping huge.

"What...is...is that...THAT, THAT THING? What in God's name is that, Idris? Why is that on your Umbrella?" Idris was certainly confused at this display; his brother was too stupid to be this talented in trickery. He must have had done something with the umbrella, but not this.

"I thought you did this," Idris said.
"Me? Why would I do this? I don't hurt people, or want to, that's you little killing boy...I mean I had stuck your umbrella in the ground upside down with the fabric all spreading out, but not this!"

"Why did you do that to my umbrella?" A very upset Idris asks.

"Because it is dumb, I don't know...you have to get rid of this now!"

"I am going to, will you help me?," Idris asks.

"I can't...it's too dirty...I can't...," and with his words trailing off Mikhail turns around and starts slowly running and sobbing with his head down, stopped in his path to vomit and then picking up pace again, yelling as he runs and cries, "JUST GET RID OF IT...IT'S GROSS, IDRIS!...IDRIS, IT'S SICK!..."

Idris wraps it up as he was pointlessly interrupted, but a bit relieved to know that he will not have to kill his brother. He heads to the water to dump it. When he gets there he cannot bring himself to do it because all of the fish are staring at him with their obscenely puckered mouths and jutting eyeballs, looking pitiful and not able to deal with sharing their home with a severed head. He did drop it once in a shallow part where there seemed to be no sign of little fishes, but a turtle came up from behind him on the land and looked at him to inform him that what he just did should be reversed. Idris conceded.

Something about Idris is if things are nice to him he will

be nice back, unless he thinks they might try to kill him, then he will want to kill them first. Aminah, the nanny whose brother's skull he was trying to discard would always tell him that he was mean, and he would say that that was impossible because there was no reason to be as such. He was a reputable boy in this historical city of Baghdad.

As we were discussing Idris he reached another possible place where he might release this traveling head. He walked to the populated area of the Bazaar and just dropped it between people's trampling feet where he witnessed it immediately being kicked about the area, and not noticed, like rotten fallen fruit, or bread, or something. Maybe a beggar will pick it up and eat it.

A soldier of higher rank called him over and told him that he looked ridiculous walking about in his sleeping uniform, and that he must be up to no good. Idris told the high ranking official that this is not the situation, but he was good, and also a soldier, and always walked around like this, for it was the new style of his patriotic Battalion. The soldier with his weapon gripped tight told the boy that he was a bad thief, and that he should give back what he stole. Idris said that he was not aware of what he was talking about, and possibly, he will commend him to his chief for being so stern, and unshakable. The soldier said that he could be no more praised this month than he already was. The soldier said to Idris that he wants the story now. Idris started crying and there is nothing left to say. Well, I will say that I am not saying that Idris said anything else at all; he may just have cried and walked away, or maybe something else. Possibly he did steal something after he dropped the head and we just do not know of it. I do not know...

II

Aminah woke up and saw a letter under her door informing her that her brother had been killed, his body found, but head missing. She started crying in her moderate manner that she was accustomed to for dead brothers.

Aminah was a nanny to many little boys, but had no little boys. Now all her brothers have been successfully shot. She was referred to as sister of boys, and mother of boys, from the boys she nannied. She also liked the title and referred to herself in this way. Now that she has no brothers she will only be "mother of boys." She always took great care of her hair, but hid it in a hijab waiting the day until she could reveal it for husband. But, now that she did not have brothers to look for a spouse for her, or a father, anybody will feel that they can come for her seeing that there is no man to offer her hand and protect her. If she had her brother's head, at least she could place it in front of the house and warn away suitors that are afraid and weak, and who do not really want her anyway.

Aminah went to the bread shop for bread.

"How much is your cheapest, best bread?" asks the obscenely beautiful Aminah.

"Aaahh, this girl...girl says things! It speaks! Speaks, too," a seated baking woman says shaking her fat head to somewhere above her gesticulating all about.

"But does it reply?," another fat head, never betraying her eyes from the listless clump she is molding cynically mumbles.

"Does she reply!... does she reply?" dropping its voice

many loaves at the second query fat head one seems to have faded introspective wandering its tiny baby eyes spherically pivoting on the unseen in its sockets eventually terminating in bouncing vision-echoes off the bones in her inner-skull.

"Someone has died, and umm...uuhh...you see, my own family, and you people, ladies, sisters...sisters of our faith?...my last brother...my last brother to be killed, insha-Allah. No money I have...no, some money, but little money... more money soon, yes, yes...but no now money, see?" says her.

"How money soon?," with which a positively small head on a definitely fat neck introduces herself. She has all the suggestions of leadership about her.

"There is always work for the girl with no brothers."

"AAAAHHHHHH," says all baking things.

"mm-hmm," a baking woman.

"SURE," a baking woman.

"Why not?," a baking woman.

"I would say so myself if things...," a baking woman.

"This is how the...," a baking woman.

"sounds about right," a baking woman.

"Yes, yes, that is okay," a last baking woman.

As all this was happening mother Aminah saw the head floating in the air outside and fly into the Masjid. Aminah ran after it and approached it. She told it to come back, and asked it if it would help her at least get a husband. It pretended to not understand. She started sobbing explaining all her past woes and present ones, even explaining that she couldn't even get a stupid piece of bread from all the fat and ugly-haired bread women, but when she looked up, the head was gone. Must have flown away, and with today's wind, must have gone far.

She went to the army, but they said they couldn't help. She did all sorts of things. One day a high ranking soldier brought the head back to her. He asked her if it was hers, and she said no, but it belonged to her. He gave it back, and she did a favor for him.

She did have the body with her too and tried to get a mortician to put it back on so she could put the whole body out front but nothing would work because the body was rotted so. She actually ran into the man that she wanted to marry with his mother and found them to be treating her quite strangely indeed. She asked them why, and they said they didn't know what she was talking about but that they all found her to be wonderful and definitely a possible wife for the man. This delighted her and made her realize that she did not need to have the head or the body with the head of her brother in front of the house to get a decent husband.

III

The next day she woke up and her brother's body with his head on it was out front as he used to be when they would have a possible suitor come to the house. She looked again to make sure she was seeing correctly. It was there. She even asked her neighbor if she saw the handsome man and the woman said that she had seen a handsome man.

Idris came over for his weekend visit to stay with his nanny Aminah and he was shocked when he saw the head on the dead body out front. That day, when they came back from the Masjid and he brushed her hair, he told her that he thought she was pretty, and she kissed him on the nose.

19

Watching

"This is the glory of the Heavens…of the Divine," said the angel to the young writer, ugly in his true form, with both palms facing the pitch fog above, and eyes twitching in a seizure from trying to observe every one of the thousand scenes of brutality occurring concurrently. The writer watches the angel watch; the angel seems to be watching one scene in particular that involved a torturer with a gigantic metal mouth and a woman. This sort of torture must be more dear to it than others. The writer seems to think it a bit queer, though, the juvenile excitement the angel cannot contain when observing the similar torturous punishments it has been watching over, and directing for some hundreds of years now. Being nobody special on Earth, really, the writer thought that it would be quite silly of him to not visit possibly the most vivid place to a human's knowledge when his God offered. "And certainly there would be something to write about there," he thought.

Actually, many people were invited- any angel who wanted to attend, prophets, philosophers, artists, some common men on Earth, and more. He was the only person who seemed to care, and the care was more self-serving, because the angel and himself were the only in attendance. The Heavens, its God who suggested he go, and the angel's peers there, certainly did not care enough to attend. The one scene out of many that the angel fixated on suddenly ascended to the same height as the ground of the hill the writer and angel stood upon. The spectacle was directly in front of them now and the angel put both his hands together as if to clap, but just jiggled and shook them with his befittingly bouncing up and down delighted giant body; the loose grin that the writer has seen on its face since arrival became a bit more tight, rigid, and definite, as if it new it would be in this countenance for some time so it would be better to make it permanent. It almost seemed as if this was a surprise for it, a present; but the worker angel who had the gigantic jaws, and was the torturer of this woman, in the scene now before them stopped its work and straightened its posture, steadied its eyes in front, and remained still for the angel as if this was a common procedure with our high ranking angel. The angel looked at the writer and made a sweeping gesture with his arm and held it with fingers pointing at the scene suggesting an invitation to walk on the blood and flesh-smeared platform and inspect.

Since the raising of the scene, seemingly arranged by the angel, most likely raised for the purpose of trying to get the writer as fascinated as it was, it felt as if the many different scenes happening below, in the distance, were not in existence, just a background with small moving figures from where occasional screams escape. Nothing truly existed at this moment with exception to the smooth-faced stringy blond-haired writer, two-story high grotesque angel, the damned bald-headed woman with a mouth horrifically descended and puckered simultaneously and apparently stuck with it, but eyes that said she he had a vague idea of who she is, was, and where. And also existing in this moment was the still standing erect punishing angel who moments ago had slowly chewed off a section of the woman's labia, which would explain a hanging and mangled bloody piece of soft flesh dangling in front of her and partly resting on the platform she was sitting on with her legs straight out and spread, but back straight as the big-mouthed worker angel. If the writer listened to the stamped expression of terror on her face that has not moved he may feel sympathy, but because those lips do not move, and because of her pleasant blue eyes saying "whoever was here before vanished," he is just as moved as her mouth.

The writer was not as delighted as the angel with the metal mouth, but thought the woman a bit attractive, and particularly grew fond of the disfigured mouth. Not really worried about the reaction of the woman to him strolling around her and stopping to inspect her recent torture, he poked her in different parts questioning the physical state of existence that one is in here. The angel could not help itself from stepping over to the big mouth and adjusting some screws and mechanical malfunctions. It separated the metal jaws to where the top of the back of the worker angel's head touched its spine; it seemed that it took pride in checking and fixing these things itself, although surely an angel of the lower order should be tending to such menial trifles.

The angel stepped back from the open mouth, as the worker angel knew better than to shut it until it was told as such, and shifting in different positions closing one eye or the other it said with a euphoric tremble in his voice, "Oh, Majestic Creator." Apparently, this was as effective as any signal for the worker to shut his big mouth. "It really is frighteningly cold here," said the writer, still attempting to make positive the vacancy of the soul of the woman by looking in her eyes with very similar motions the angel had when stepping back from the open mouth. The angel looked at the writer with disgust as the writer continued to study the woman, perhaps from his interest in her and not the mouth, or at least the background violence.

"That depends on the scene you are watching...it is all environmental...and when here for so long, when We look at everything together, all visions of our Lord's Mercy, Justice, Love, it feels as being close to the presence of the Most Beautiful...you kind of feel it watching her, but, if you really focus on the precision of a Heavenly built machine, just as she is, or you, even I, ...but one that cannot corrupt, or be corrupted, although I am designed to do as He says...these little and big wonders are the most masterful creation, they only act on their design, nothing more.... they are innocents."

20

Burning Buildings

Fogs of the gray gravel dust clouds swirl opposite from the direction of the vehicle that created it. Catherine's eyeballs bulge at seeing the vast stretches of concrete and fenced in squares of rubble. She becomes aware of her tiny eyes in comparison to the many empty big holes in dirty buildings speckled all around, and within, the pavement.

I know this will all end badly. Probably, I will be humiliated somehow; she will appear as if victorious, and I as victim, yet she will still be showered with sympathy. They will all hate me even more. Nadine will think me horrible, Ivan will want to stab me, and the rest will just hate me normally. She is waiting for my limit. She thinks I will reveal it with mild anger, and then she can take control and design my ruin from then on. But possibly it will be like -

Oh Catherine,

Hello, dear, just saying hello. I hope you see this. I left it on the fridge because I remember you saying that you wanted to finish the fruits and you were going to eat it for breakfast today. I cut them up for you and peeled them. I did enjoy yesterday. I just really like you, much. I am so happy about us, and the friends we have, and our house, and life. Isn't it wonderful? It will continue forever, as long as you want, lovely. You deserve it. You really do. Oh, how much I am enjoying all this. See you very soon.

Love you - Love you,
Edward

Edward pulls into the dirt lot where Catherine directed him to with the buildings near it. Catherine begins pulling off her panties and hiking up her dress expressly in the passenger seat. She does not look at Edward's face as she takes out his cock mechanically. Edward is with arms raised and palms facing the front window; he is frozen as if something is happening to him that he has no control over. Catherine shoves her left palm in his face trying to grip it whilst handling his genitals roughly with the long glossy nails of her right hand. Edward is a little more tense now, barely shifting, tossing his gaze about the ceiling of the car and not knowing where to put his hands, moving them slowly and timidly.

Random garbage camouflaged vagabonds come out of the deserted buildings toward the car. One tramp is moving faster than the others. He has one leg and he is hopping fast.

They are all a particular shade of darkness, which looks queer moving about speedily in this attacking sun shine. The one leg hopper has blue eyes that shove out of the smear-colored face skin. Very hard to distinguish skin from garments due to similarity of texture and color, but at closer encounter it is apparent that these people are very modest and cover their bodies quite severely.

Catherine struggles with the levers adjusting Edward's chair back more than he already set it, and she does this with a sense of panic that seems relative to the quickly advancing swarthy men. Covering Edward's cock with a tall hollow metal phallus, she lowers her cunt onto it. All the seats have been covered with sheets. Catherine presses a button and all the windows roll down. Edward turns his face to the driver-side door as he is all the way reclined on the chair.

Edward's nose is getting shoved into the inside door handle from Catherine's now slamming descent on phallus. His eyes are open and watching his nose tip hit the leather handle in rhythm but it is a watching that has no afterthoughts or influence. He does not know what is happening to his body if something other than what has been told is happening. The men who have arrived outside the driver's side window and are seemingly just standing as we see them from inside the car are seeing Catherine's hands violently knead the side of his head with her knuckles making his hair swirl and stick out in one particular area.

The one-legged tramp is also in front of the driver-side window with his penis out, and still hopping for balance he is masturbating with cock pointed toward a moderately small opening in the window. All the other late-to-get-up, a little more unhealthy and less ambitious appear, all pulling out their penises and getting in front of one of the four window openings respective of their positions. All assume a variety of different countenances. Some have tongues out, but as a habitual gesture and not connotative, one is squinting eyes and mouth alternately, probably an after effect from the realm of concentration, and the hopper, who must be chafing himself with his wiry wool coverings wrapped around hands steadily pulls and pushes his cock skin to and fro with one hand as the other steadily wipes his eyes and then rubs the corner of his mouth, all the while hopping on his one leg.

Catherine puts out both of her hands toward the window as an indicating gesture while still bounce squatting on apparatus. Hands, many and different, but all in fist form, invade the inside of the car as deep as they can before their forearms are squeezed by the window's glass edge. They are competing to hand Catherine lumps of the dirty dirt interspersed with garbage and glass. She takes it without looking at the donors' faces and shovels it into Edward's mouth, packing the excess about to spill with firm pats that slap his limp lips. Edward's eyes face the plush burgundy cloth lined ceiling. With Edward's head tilted back as such one of the still masturbating men who has been watching Edward from the beginning is very impressed by the aquiline Adam's apple bulging up high that could give any nose a good competition. Some infidels within the men's group are only interested in watching the boys Catherine brings rather than receiving the gift she bestows upon them; these are the same who have misused the theory of *her* needing them in order to have the power to grant such blessings. The theory was just to promote responsibility and pride among the men and to combat the idea of being utterly dependent upon her. It does not mean that they have the power to kill her by not giving attention, she will just go reward men elsewhere. The chosen will always test her the most because of feelings of jealousy toward other groups; they want the most proofs and signs and reminders of being chosen. Not fair, really.

Edward's mouth is trickling a mixture of saliva, dirt and blood down his chin with eyes trembling a bit but still not betraying anything felt.

The vagabonds all shoot their semen toward open window within the same 25 seconds. One-third of the semen accomplishes the interior of the car, while one-half of that one-third plop on the bodies in the car, much on the driver side cheek of Catherine. The one-legged tramp is furiously trying to ejaculate, though; he hops closer to the window moving his head about attempting to catch sight of something that might rouse him. His penis is halfway erect, sad, like a soggy branch maybe.

Catherine looks at the One-legged tramp with a sincerely concerned expression. He is madly bouncing around the entire car frantic, looking for something inside to empower him. All vagabonds are concerned as well and move toward him, caressing him lovingly, trying to calm his jumping about. He is surrounded by caressers to the extent that he cannot hop anywhere but just move his upper body and head from side to side, lower and higher trying to glimpse a thing more explicit and invigorating as he is stubbornly yanking on the unreceptive flesh that would love nothing more than to just dangle unobstructed. He appears annoyed by these soothers who are restricting him. Catherine tries to lift a leg up a little bit higher, still looking very concerned , so that he may see a wet labia side, or something.

Shrinking from the irritating touches One-leg falls to the ground. They lower themselves as far as needed to still caress him as if nothing has interrupted the flow of touching. Catherine is outside now and petting him, as well. Pigeons and dogs and rats all flock to him pecking and licking and nibbling. His penis is completely soft and he is done with it but he is smiling a little. Edward is blankly wiping off the metal phallus with a cleaner and rag that Catherine brought along because asked him to do as such very politely. He is okay, really.

Children are playing and laughing in front of the buildings, which are now burning. The children are mimicking all the scenes that have occurred before them. A little girl is playing Edward. A little girl with her leg visibly tied behind her is playing One-legged tramp.

21

Queen Aghastiantra

I went to watch the sewer-grate girl walk three steps lengthwise and four tiny steps adjacent to the width of the oblong cavity that says "SewerGrate." Her naked, Lilliputian feet, susceptible to all the filth that hovers and falls from things queer above onto the porous ground that we stomp arrogantly with our rigid foot-fortifications, escape vitreous, smooth, impervious. I did not see her toes move. No longer shall I believe that her feet even touch the sullied ground. They do levitate the height of a baby moth standing upright on its hind legs, tummy exposed. The only doubt lies in the inaction of not laying my head with ear to concrete so as to give me the vantage view needed to exact this not phantasm. I am not rude. And she has been kind enough to appear stolid to my stares at her circumambulations around the striated vacuum where waste is, giving me a thing wonderful for my horrid, big eyes. I gaze, not gawk, yes. I do try to stand at the same place when I am compelled to go there so as to not disrupt the dizzy calm. It is difficult because the only fixed objects are sewer-grate girl and sewer-grate. Crossing the threshold whence I came-- Behold!--a comfortably bleak stretch, smears graduating to resolute horizons terminating in vanishing points that promise the same funeral of the senses were I to skip thither.

At toes' first touch on girl besprinkled tract the intermezzo takes twenty-two metrical steps to come upon, or seemingly upon because it is hard to be positive, my mezzanine proper where the pink-clad girl's ambulatory floating can be enjoyed detached. After I see her it becomes possible to leave plane. A quantitatively expressed tramp is revealed to me when it is time for me to know so I may cross back over the twinkling, conterminous border. Revealed numbers vary. Little choice in regard to motion when numbers are implanted; I am too frightened to resist as of yet. The presence of terror when fleeing is not imparted by her, but numbers may be. It is from without us twain. She has been only most passively kind and receptive of our tacitly agreed distance in tableau. She must be foreign to such a bitter grate, her being all pink and queerly wafting about. I do not move forward implying motion toward her, or the hole she circles, past my respective spot(s); I do move sideways or retrograde for escape from ominous feeling that is not from her or I. Nasty invisible that compels me to uncouthly flit somewhere otherly from girl; sympathetic girl giving the numbers so at least I may return whence I began.

She wears the pink sticky material stained with soot, menses and shit. Not ancient pink but urgent, obscene pink.

I suppose she effects her significant stools devoid of my eyes. I worry about it because I would be simply horrified if I were the cause impelling her to possess something she should dispel. Her little pink shorts and strangling bodice strangling her will never harmonize with skin and faggot-ash-black tress in a classical sense but she makes her statement well. I do see her pee and bleed from her tiny bulge through the pink. Bulging from a reaching out not an intruding in. She is smaller than me but both our breasts are irreducibly juvenile. Hers are harder. Adamantine but destructible. Maybe ours touching would be as metal scraping ice-- hers metal, mine ice. I understand the distension in her cunt as being familial with my little bump. My bulge more bitter, brutal; hers detached, wondrous object, gooey curio. Maybe ours touching is as when blood floats on milk; hers milk, mine blood. And the line of separation/connection is the bitterness I contain toward something otherly and hers the insouciance at something she owns but will not own. And like mine hers should be grazed and rigorously rubbed not pierced, irrupted.

The violent pink uninterrupted tracts on those shorts effete to gossamer between her holes. Yes, a withering cloth track, I will say beginning, from the linear dent betwixt her rear impressed by the pressure imposed from her squalid little humps. It extends to and vanishes within the neglected, supple fleshland that suggests a third chamber-- the limbo span a louse must traverse from the harsh plexus of pubic confusion to the delicate wisps of hair adorning the asshole; the Red and Black ant's zenith. A forsaken nexus where chafed pink struggles by tenuous threads latching on to the left and right moments of flaccid pink inner thighs so as to not be subdued into the amassing collective absence of crotch. Suddenly reemerging from the quasi-moth hostility onto the aplenty whole pink calm it is only distressed by a tiny bump who says "cunt." And eventually-- synthesis with smiling pink facade made viable by the flatness of her boyish pelvis. A thing said about pink in grey is that it is death in truth. And pink circling holes-- a beacon lest you trample and fall.

We have heavy Siberian Black hair, long and wicked. We have Horrid Big eyes because there is something wrong with us. We have Purgatory Grey irises, though my pupils are perennially contracted inherited from my lulled, decaying father. We have the Wandering Arab skin stretched on brittle body. We have wistful hair above our Suffocated Blue Dry lips implying a smear of dirt. We have an arch shoving our lower back forward saying we are either offering our little belly or our little butt but I think we are not. We have the Mongolian Purple aureoles besieging the Sudanese Purple nipples sur-mounting boyish bumps. Her cunt is filthy, mine smells; hers suggests love, mine boredom. Our mouth is wide and queer and lurid. I have one fang among my upper teeth. It is on the left. I tease it with my tongue. Our face is religiously pretty though the whole theme synthesized with our body exalts us to a thing profane. Other people look quite perverse and different.

I announce to every bug moving that I do not care for this stupid floating girl. She is being watched. I can only offer her the peasantland smiles of a penniless horizon. I have a goat-smeared future untouched by her circular prayers. We cannot mingle; I will bring her down.

She knows nothing of my diseased ways. I have the ability

to do things. I will find something rod-like and beat her for her own heavenly guarantee. She may not agree but she knows other people know much more. And her blood can spray and shower giggling, grateful mothers who need to bathe their dumb bodies as well. I wish you plenty, much, idiot girl, on the day you arrive to the place you are not going.

CANTO 4

PINK TREES

22

The Pink Trees

INT. FILTHY BATHROOM -- DAYLIGHT THROUGH WINDOW.

CU *wretched bathtub floor with shower water spilling over Ivan's feet; drain is a bit clogged and water is three inches backed up. There is no sound except hollow, fitful nasal inhaling and exhaling as it sounds within the ears of the person breathing..*

Nadine defecating on toilet perpendicular, and front rim very close, to bathtub edge. Seeing feces descend from view between top of Nadine's thighs. Her knees are chafed. Panties are severely shiny white intermittently imbued with speckles of pinkish dried blood stretched just below knees. Seeing her pee on top of still feces in shallow toilet water. She has socks pulled up to just below her knees

Seeing water in tub, Ivan's feet.

CU semen floating on bathtub water. One strand clinging to his ankles. All sounds pertinent to environment audible now including shower on backed-up water, toilet flushing and Nadine talking.

NADINE

... just beautiful. She is really pretty. I like her face when she is a bit disgusted. Probably because she's not really disgusted. I don't know. If I felt that she was really disgusted it would just seem that I couldn't possibly enjoy her ... being uncomfortable.

Nadine wetting tissue with toilet water and wiping her crotch first and then ass with the same tissue.

I know some enjoy that and there is nothing wrong with that at all but I know I could not find her being sickened... or you know, being disturbed -- pleasurable... beautiful. I'm just not like that. Nothing is wrong with it but I would be too worried about trying to make her feel better. Why do

Nadine grabs dry tissue and wipes ass first and then crotch, un-intentionally, from confusion of the proper order of holes. Stands up and pulls up panties attempting to scratch off blood stains but gives up fast and complacently. She washes hands but does not use soap next to sink.

you think about it. You ask me almost weekly about seeing her face, seeing her face "mooove".

IVAN

He is mumbling to himself inaudible to Nadine. Seeing him wash his body randomly but always returning to wash genitals after every body part. Not seeing his face.

(mumbles)

The bathtub knows me as nothing more than the furtive monster with loud feet. It is fine. But, when a day appears, if another day appears...

NADINE

What'd you say, babe? I know you are not talking to me when you talk like that but I ask you anyway in case you are and I just can't hear you. See how wonderful I can be? So .... I think tonight is going to be good; Edward said Catherine got her hair cut yesterday, I can't imagine what she looks like. Babe, how much longer you think you need? I do need to wash up still. Or do you want me to come in there with you? Would you like that?

CU Ivan's disgruntled face making contortions of the mouth as if he tastes something bitter. CU of lips as he mumbles.

IVAN

(mumbles)

wench that utters violates the pores of walls twirling
language that leaks disease to the innocent.

(to Nadine)

I'm coming out now. How did she get her hair cut?

NADINE

(confused, then annoyed)

How?... I'm not sure, babe; different? Edward said she looked
different. I'm sure she looks great.

(laughs, a bit scornfully)

So you're coming out.

Ivan steps out of the shower cupping his genitals not looking at
Nadine as she follows him with her eyes and a smirk of wonder. He
brushes past her.

IVAN

Excuse me.

(wraps towel around torso, tucking ends in tight and leaves bathroom)

(mumbles)

I am as bad as you sick little girl touching everything inconsiderate. I should touch you inconsiderate. I touch me
inconsiderate, horrible, with strangeness.

INT. APARTMENT -- DAYLIGHT BRIGHT

*Seeing immaculate apartment and hearing some pretty electronic
music playing. Ivan goes expressly to the stereo and turns it off.*

*Seeing Nadine in the shower washing herself but using wrong
products for wrong parts out of her large assortment. Ivan's semen
strand clinging to her ankles in backed up muddled water.*

*Ivan slips on underwear in effeminate manner under towel and then
removes towel and looks at his clothes.*

IVAN

(mumbles)

what has a man to do with vanity? his origin is semen and his end is a carcass, while he cannot feed himself nor ward off death.

(Looks at his hands and feet and penis, clacks and grinds teeth. Shivers willy-nilly and stretches arms down tautly with palms facing floor so to control his body.)

all these parts.

(Shakes torso willfully watching penis and testicles jiggle. Suddenly stops and pulls underwear up tight and shakes slightly making sure jiggling has ceased.)

EXT. INDUSTRIAL AREA -- DAY

Car speeding on road in deserted area. Pulls in to open lot.

INT. CAR -- DAY

Catherine pulling off her panties and hiking up her dress with celerity in passenger seat. Not looking at Edward's face as she takes out his dick vehemently. Edward with arms raised and palms facing front window; he is frozen as if something is happening to him that he has no control over. Catherine shoves her left palm in his face trying to grip it whilst handling his genitals roughly. Edward is a little more tense now, not knowing where to put his hands moving them about slowly and timidly.

EXT. INDUSTRIAL AREA -- DAY

Random vagabonds come out of divers abandoned buildings toward car. One tramp is moving faster than the others. He has one leg and he is hopping fast. They are all seemingly black..

INT. CAR -- DAY

Catherine struggles with the levers adjusting Edward's chair back hurriedly. She attaches a metal apparatus to his dick and puts it into her vagina. All the seats are covered with sheets. Catherine presses a button and all the windows roll down. Edward turns his face to the driver-side door as he is all the way reclined on the chair.

CU Edward's face from door angle. His eyes are open but he looks detached from what is happening to his body. We can see Catherine's hands kneading the side of his head harshly from the same shot.

EXT. OUTSIDE OF CAR -- DAY

One-legged tramp is in front of driver-side window with his penis out still hopping for balance and he is masturbating with dick pointed toward opening in window. The other vagabonds appear, about five, all pulling out their penises and getting in front of window openings respective of their positions. All assume fairly ambiguous countenances.

INT. CAR -- DAY

Catherine puts out both of her hands toward window while still getting penetrated by dick + apparatus. Vagabonds' hands seen inside car handing Catherine lumps of the dirty dirt interspersed with garbage and glass. She takes it without looking at them and shoves it into Edward's mouth as he is still gazing at nothing toward the door.

CU Edward's mouth trickling a mixture of saliva, dirt and blood down his chin with eyes jittering a bit but still empty.

EXT. OUTSIDE CAR -- DAY

Vagabonds ejaculate toward open window. One-legged tramp furiously trying to ejaculate; he gets closer to window moving his head about attempting to catch sight of something that might rouse him. His dick is halfway erect.

INT. CAR -- DAY

Some semen still darting through window opening onto various areas including Catherine and Edward. Catherine looks at One-legged tramp with sincerely concerned expression. He is hopping about the car frenetically looking for something inside. All vagabonds are concerned as well and move toward him, caressing him lovingly trying to soothe his frustration.

EXT. OUTSIDE CAR -- DAY

Vagabonds caressing One-legged tramp. He shrinks from their touches yet they still persist. He falls to ground and they are still caressing him. Catherine is petting him now as well. Pigeons and dogs and rats all flock to him pecking and licking and nibbling. His penis is completely soft now but he is smiling a little.

Children are seen playing and laughing in corner of screen in front of burning buildings. The children are mimicking all the scenes that have occurred before them. A little girl is playing Edward. A little girl with her leg visibly tied behind her is playing One-legged tramp.

INT. EDWARD AND CATHERINE'S APARTMENT -- NIGHT

A sense of emptiness pervades the apartment's living room. There are a few objects that suggest an attempt to make the apartment appear as if comfortably living people reside within. Objects that Catherine believes through memory she saw in other people's homes. They look queer amongst the milieu, though. Possibly from the way they are placed, possibly because the objects appear queer to Catherine herself and she feels utterly foreign from them and their related realm.

Seeing Catherine, Edward, Ivan, and Nadine sitting in the living room. Catherine is sitting in a small, hard chair next to Edward who is seated in a relatively large cushioned chair(he is in the position that one would assume if one were seemingly relaxed with their back against the inner back of the chair, but if viewed closer his back is not actually touching the cushion). Ivan is sitting on the low couch with his knees quite high because of his long legs; Nadine is next to him leaning a bit toward him with her shoulder and she is smiling to an acceptable limit.

NADINE

Your hair! You look like you think about things... things you didn't look like you thought before. How is it for you, Edward?

CATHERINE

Oh, I think about things... less things and different. Things have more angles now, not just silly and everywhere. Edward likes it, yes.

NADINE

So here it is, Ivan... well, how do you feel about it?

(Facing Catherine.)

He has been thinking of it ever since I mentioned it happened.

IVAN

Why do you say such things? I have thought about it, but only as much as any image one introduces to another from words. I do not decide to think about these kinds of things but it is reactionary to the words spoken ... I cannot help it. You told me about it. It is how ears to brain interact. Why would you say that? As if I am thinking about how I feel about it; I am sure I feel something about it, like every image I take a thousand times a second. It is so rude of you to make me appear foreign from everybody else's way of thinking. You should not speak as such.

(Catherine smiles complaisantly.)

CATHERINE

Do you enjoy it, though... Ivan?

Ivan turns to look at Catherine as if with courage but looks down when he sees her staring at him with her sure grin. This is the first time Ivan has even attempted to look at anybody.

IVAN

As much as anything, possibly.

(mumbles)

dead boys have nastiest tongues as well.

NADINE

(Laughing wide-eyed at Catherine in awe of her as if something
was uttered that is heavier than now allows.)

Enjoy? Oh, Catherine, you are a dirty woman. Enjoy! You
would really say that! You said that to him.

CATHERINE

Ivan? Enjoy-enjoy-enjoy-enjoy. Ivan, will you enjoy it? Much?

IVAN

Yes.

(Not looking at anybody or objects, with hands on knees.

CATHERINE

Oh, Ivan, I would love for you to think about it much... My hair. As much as you need to. You should be able to... Unrestrained. I declare that my permission has been granted to you, a man, to think about my hair much, as much as needed.

Ivan does not seem affected by these words in movement. He dominantly remains the same as pre-permission. There is something in his face, though, that indicates that he may have been affected by it, and possibly reluctantly content by it.

NADINE

(Sincerely)

Ivan, did you hear that? That is so sweet, Catherine. Did you hear that, Ivan? Did you hear that, Edward? That is so sweet, Catherine. A wonderful thing to say.

(Shaking her head to herself looking down in amazement.)

Yeah, it really is. Edward?

Catherine turns her head slowly to sharply look at Edward constricting his reply.

EDWARD

(Suddenly realizing he's expected to reply, he readjusts his posture and effects a series of slightly contorted countenances.)

It is nice.

(He looks to Catherine self-conscious and hesitant.)

A nice thing to say.

CATHERINE

(She shows Edward a bitter half-smile and then turns head towards Nadine with celerity.)

Thank you, Nadine, Edward, but I am not trying to be nice. Honestly, I just want him to think of it freely. It is so difficult these days...everything...please, Ivan, please, you should. You should be able to...it's not fair.

(She self-consciously glances at Edward and he puts his head down ashamed.)

23

Coughing

Characters
Girl
Boy 1
Boy 2
Waiter
Elderly Smoking Women
Waitress
Asthmatic Boys
Man - Asthmatic boys' father

ACT I

Inside of a 24 hour diner sits three people in the smoking section waiting for their food. There are two boys and one girl. Sexuality is ambiguous, though age is definitely early twenties, possibly even late teens. There is no mood of seriousness about them, but rather light-hearted capriciousness.

Boy 1:

Oh yeah, I remember now...anyway, we don't talk anymore, anyway.

Girl:

[Coughs]

The cough seems to have suggested themes of human frailty, sickness, mortality, because the need to avoid such thoughts by the group right now is so desperate that what follows is an awkward loudly observed set of fumbling silverware, a burst of compulsive finger drumming, asses shifting in polyurethane seats, and one solitary intake of breath loud enough that for a moment they all flinch from their own human skin, but are abruptly escorted to safety by the voice of Boy 1 speaking.

Boy 1:

We have a closet, but the door is broken.

They pause after hearing it, even the boy whose words it was, before they allow themselves to wholly immerse in their diner booth environment again.

Boy 2:

I swear to God I didn't do it but I saw it...I saw this psycho girl do it.

The waiter arrives at the group's table with three plates and places the correct food in front of the correct diner. He then stands for a moment until the group has a peek at him.

Boy 1:

[To Boy 2]

That's a lot of Bacon.

The waiter glides to the table again, hands clasped in front of his long torso, head humbly tilted.

Girl:

[To Waiter]

Do you know Maria?

Waiter:

Yeeaah!

[Now very matter-of-factly]

She comes in here every day. She is always late. She says she can see the diner from her apartment.

Girl:

Yeah.

She shifts her eyes to her plate and begins to adjust her body as if she is preparing for a new task, and informing the old one that she is finished.

Waiter walks away. The group is eating their food in the manner of many who treat it as medicine and is better when finished rather than during. All their heads are bowed to the plate with cheeks puffing and contracting. Each is focused enough on getting done that they are not bothered by each other's noises. Their own eating sounds are so loud in their head that they can barely hear a shout, they think. Waiter appears with even stronger smiling eyes, a shinier forehead, taller, thicker hair, maybe even more teeth.

Waiter:

Sooo, how is everybody doing?!

All the group look up to him at the same time with obscenely stuffed mouths stopped.

Boy 1, Boy 2, Girl:

[All together, heads nodding]

Mmmm-hmmm.

Waiter:

[Bubbling with power]

GREEAAT!

The waiter flits elsewhere. The group watches him with another table as they slowly begin to chew at the same rate with which they are coming out from under his lingering heat. They are abruptly sobered when the waitress leads two severely elderly women to a whole booth two down from them. They watch in shock as the women take their time removing their outer-wear and seating themselves. Boy 3 cannot endure to finish watching the woman who took a bit longer than the first to sit. He attempts to sway the rest of the group from this sight by really slamming his metal fork into the ceramic plate. Girl does not move a thing but her eyes to glance at the remaining food, and then back to the woman who in that briefly skipped moment by Girl sat to completion. Once seated the two women had lit all white cigarettes and dropped their thin shoulders some inches. They heard the waiter's voice approaching and they all suddenly tried to appear as if they still had the fervor to finish their food.

Waiter:

[Muscles a bit more taut, darker skinned, in a bewitching form-fitted suit, deeper voiced]

DOING GOOD, YES! YES, DOING GOOD!

The waiter leaps to the other side of the diner as the group watches on and begins to feel fear toward him.

Girl:

[Staring at her food]

I am fine...I mean I don't need this anymore...we need somebody to take all of it...like, really very soon.

*She glances about the diner looking for a waiter, but not theirs, or
busboy, manager, anything.*

*The boys both stopped eating immediately after Girl declared the
end. They were all quite helpless looking around, over their shoulders, at the elderly smoking women, even accidentally at their
waiter once though they quickly pretended to be looking behind him,
beside him, anywhere near him but not him. As they were twisting
and stretching their necks all around and raised a bit higher by sitting on their knees atop the booth seats their gaze was steadied once
more by the hostess delivering three boys all with irritated blue lips.
She sat them in the booth between the group and the old women.
Sitting, they all pulled out burgundy asthma pumps and set them
on the table; they did not even look at the pumps or each other. The
waitress leaned over so that her head would be more at their level.*

Waitress:

[With pathetic voice]

Wouldn't you boys rather sit in non-smoking seeing as the
smoke might bother your little lungs?

*She looked to all their faces individually with a pout and her hands
at her waist.*

They did not look at her but all simultaneously pointed to a man approaching their table who brushed the waitress away with his hand and seated himself.

Man:

[To the waitress]

Oh, they givin' you problems?...They're my boys! Thanks for seating them, I just got sidetracked by the headline on the newspapers in front. You got matches? I collect matches, you know. All sorts of designs and stuff. Just a hobby, you know.

He lights a cigarette with matches though he split's the match in half and puts the other half back inside the matchbook.

Waitress:

[Smiling at the children and standing now but still with her hands on her waist]

I'll see what I can do, sir...and I will definitely see if I can't get you guys a little treat!

The boys all look to each other with strange eyes and make an expression with their mouth that suggests an attempt to smile/

I think I see a little tiny smiley-smile! I think I do! I really, really do! I'll be right back to take your orders, sir, and you boys finish all your dinner so that you can get your treat from me.

The waitress shuffles her lewd hips toward the manager and talks quietly to him with a look of concern on her face as the manager looks toward the elderly smoking women, and then each boy. Girl, Boy 1, and Boy 2 have each ventured off on their own paths of staring. The Girl has been following a trace of aqua veins on one of the women and still tracing it through underneath the woman's clothes; Girl started feeling a tingling on her own body on the same path that she was traveling on the smoking old woman. She did stop and look at a crevice in one of the boy's blue suffocating lips. It looked dry and wet. Boy 1 noticed bumps on the boys' father's eyelids. He wanted them gone, away from this world that he is in. He would do it, he thought, but only by tearing the whole lid off and liquefying it so that no fleshy bump survived. He had no problem with the father, really, though. Just didn't want the bump around. Boy 2 only stared at the little boy with the thinnest skin under his eyes. He could see underneath that skin...really, he could, he thought. It was a bit blackish in dull light but if the boy turned a certain way it would become a bit pinkish and you could see fluid lurking beneath. Boy 2 also stared at this boy's lips; he thought it the most majestic, gorgeous. He would like this boy for himself. To have, and watch, and for rewards to himself, to examine by touch. Surely there are ways for these sorts of wants to be accommodated in this town, he thought. He never heard of anything that he could not possibly own. Their food still waited, unwanted and not needed. A trail of fire shot across the restaurant and at the end of it was the waiter at their table again, but now hovering some few feet.

Waiter:

[Taller, stronger, porcelain flesh, a young Persian boy's face, and mirror black hair, and now speaking in whispers]

Oh, sad, sad things. Oh, oh...

And as he sighs with a turn of the head, covering his eyes from the group their food disappears.

The waiter bursts into hundreds of soapy bubbles as the asthmatic boys escape from their seats toward them.

Asthmatic Boys:

TREEEATS!

The waitress escorts another set of diners to a table directly parallel to the group. They are made up of two girls and one boy. They talk loudly and randomly bouncing sentences off of ending words. The group cannot endure the sounds of this new group's voice. Boy 1 puts his jacket on, and takes it off, and repeats this rapidly and repeatedly not able to escape its cycle. Girl is moving her eyes so quickly about the elderly woman's body following the aqua vein that she is becoming dizzy. Boy 2 continues to slam into the table as he keeps on trying to get up and move toward the boy in a straight line. The new group think this old group are appalling to have to witness, and they pretend they are not there by discussing other things.

24

Fascist Installation

3 Dimensional Design
City Commissioned Art Project
Scale: 1" = 4'
Medium: concrete
Location:
Northeast corner of Chicago Ave. and Ogden Ave.

It will appear as any other hole leading to beneath the city, i.e., as a common subway entrance. It will be composed of the same materials as the street it is in and the other subway entrances catty-corner. On the corner that it is on, it will suggest its purpose as being another subway entrance. This is primarily due to the existence on all the other corners of the Chicago, Ogden, Milwaukee intersection of subway entrances that appear just as our "hole." It will be of the same textures and external aesthetics of the other subway entrances, except it will not have a raised wall ascending from the rim of the hole as do Chicago underground subway entrances. This is one distinguishing mark of its identity. It will simply be a rectangular hole with stairs descending. Because of the needed dimensions of slope in proportion to the size of the hole and average American height, half of the steps and inside will be lit from the lights on the above street that is allowed in from the size of the hole, and half will be obscured in darkness because of the amount of steps and its slope descent continuing the whole measurement of the size of the hole past the threshold of light/dark. The hole, lengthwise, will only be about half of the distance from first step to last step, as a linear path on a plane, not slope.

At the end of the steps one will have an area of ground about the size of the hole before the wall structure. The wall structure will have a directed light shining on it that is mounted on the sloped ceiling above head while on platform before wall. The light will be shining on a phone that will have simplistic instructions of where to call. There will also be video cameras and equipment relative to the technological advancement in efficient identification. This will be linked to the American Identification Computer and will be researched by its relative department. The call will take one to an automated, comforting, motherly voice that will ask questions regarding why that person, or whatever species it may be, descended the stairs into the hole.

This hole's purpose is to lure the autonomous thinker, the questioner, the foreigner who cannot notice the difference between this hole and the other subway holes.

This information of who thinks in this subversive manner

will be speculated on to find what patterns they all share, and how it can be developed to suit a more uniform structure within this country. The foreigner who is unsure of his surroundings will be identified, and a specific type of foreigner, as well. Specifically, because if this foreigner finds that he is in complete darkness and hears not a sound of subway life, and he still continues to move, he is not intimidated by the boundaries that humans have been pre-conditioned to not cross. This is the same with anybody who crosses the point where there is only darkness on the steps. This person's idea of self-satisfaction at the price of subverting and deviating from his conditioning has been decided as being the core of anti-uniformity. The preset notion of staying with the familiar and known environment is necessary for the security of national propaganda being successfully instilled without unseen questions. The boundary of the familiar to be observed by all people within these borders needs to be observed because for the government's expansion into new and more intimate territories, such as within the family home, and even the human mind, there cannot be any unexpected venturing into areas that that the government is working in. This problem can be solved with the data that will be gathered from the hole. It is placed near the other subway entrances because it is also acting as a new conditioning project that teaches to not even venture into areas that are seemingly similar and possibly familiar but different in the slightest thing. We need to be able to rely upon knowing where exactly the human can go in their own home, brain, personal thought, where they will sexually journey for satisfaction. We need to know where, and keep them only going there so that the government may exist in the intimate areas near them, but where they do not, and will not go. Even if they take some steps the darkness will send them back to the street sending a message. If it is decided that it is the most shrewd and, for best national interest, to extract the strays who make it past the dark steps all the way to the wall, it can be done just as quickly as they emerge onto the platform before the wall.

CANTO 5

PRESERVED SPECIMENS

25

Journal Entries

1.

She is just laying there, silent and sleeping. It has been a rough day for the girl-Sarah; that is too bad, really, just too bad. I like her to have a little tragedy, but in wondrous and gorgeous balloons. Ones that go up. And land in other places.

2.

Father, sister, brother going to Iraq tomorrow, actually Jordan first then Iraq. I would like to go but I cannot because the Correctional Department would rather I stay in this state for a couple more years. Understandably so. Not that I am a bad person, it is just understandably so; as are many a thing. Monkey girl-Sarah is lying on the bed on her side yawning with face toward me staring and blinking every time I look, or right after I look. I know it does not mean anything, but it could, and someday it might. And yes, today...today was a big thing happening; I had four severe panic attacks. Well, the fourth left without such a scary peak. The paramedics came and I did not go to the hospital. This is the first time I have had more than one in a day. I thought of death again, because one feels such a thing as death is quite relative to such an obscene physical occurrence. I really do not like this thing and would like it to leave with celerity/quickness/speed. I have some other problems and I think maybe that some others who need some pain should be distributed my share of this thing. I was leaking sweat into my mouth and the apartment was quite chilly, my heart felt inclined to burst and I really thought all the visceral organs I possess were going to violently exit my body through my mouth and asshole. Nothing like that came out either. In my mind there was this little ball, a sort of tiny demon ball that was doing all the bad stuff and I had to get rid of it in order for it to stop. Eventually I passed out in a chair because my body could not take anymore and when I woke the ball was gone and I looked over at the girl-Sarah who was on the same bouncy bed that she is on now and I told her "I am all better." I almost had another one later in the night. It is not as if I am upset when this thing happens to my body. School starts in a couple of weeks. I am going to concentrate on the second major more than the first this semester. I enjoy when a material drapes down making gravity so obvious and perversely needy to have control. It seems to have Eros' mark directed toward grounds and floors that beg for touch from the objects that it pulls, or pushes. I will go and touch the girl-Sarah between her legs in one moment, right after I am typing; this is something that is definite, you must trust and believe that after the last word that I will have gone over and touched her in between her legs and put a finger in her cunt, twirling it slow in circles, lovely little circles. I promise this to anybody who reads this. She will be touched within the next minute inside her, even if only now because I told you as such.

3.

Brother said he made will as we had last lunch before he was off for Iraq. He left me a bunch of things like all books, all music, life insurance to split with little brother, some say I think with artistic direction of his film work, including other objects as well. I would go to Basra and help try to reclaim our house with him, my sister (his wife), and my father but I am not legally allowed to leave this country...well...actually, I cannot even leave this city legally for two more years but I suppose that has a thing to do with the tumultuous relation-ship betwixt guns and I. I like saying *betwixt*, it is quite queer.

It is eight in the morning and I have been up since mid-night, that is when I awoke. I wanted to make dinner for the girl-Sarah before she rose because I thought she would be starving, I was, and she is always hungrier than I. I made some stuffed shells with tomato sauce and when she awoke and saw it it seemed that she was not hungry. She really likes my food but I think she was too dehydrated to eat. I want her to eat seeing that she weighs around a hundred pounds. She does have a pretty ass, though, and it is getting bigger, appearing quite exaggerated in contrast to her little tiny body. That is the sort of thing I enjoy. Yes, really, it is a thing which is deemed good by myself.

There was a time when people used to say that fucking a girl aplenty from behind would increase her ass size, or pos-sibly just fucking a girl much. This little tiny girl-Sarah's butt is getting larger, and I do fuck her very hard. She does have that arch in the back. This arch is a phenomena that occurs in my mother's genealogy, and mine as well because I have inherited it from her. Sarah has this arch from a place that is not my mother's genes, though. And a thing that can be said about this arch is that it seems for girls to be either saying that they are offering their little bellies, or their butts. For Sarah it says, **"here is my tummy with cunt below, and here is this pretty butt with hole between...do what you like."**

I am not so randy as of now but I would have nihilist sex right now; i.e., twist around my hand the hair of some kind of dirty, drugged, desperate and not so pretty thing I could go find on the street not so far away and put it in some part of her that seems conspicuously neglected, or overly abused. That just depends on her countenance, and which hole should be used in order for this situation to affect her the most, scar her the most. My wife will help me figure it all out, making suggestions and such, petting the girl and such. I am anticipating sadness, since I try to make them think that they will get something special, or more of what they asked for initially, if they assume sad weeping lilliput lost in Gigantica face. I do...actually, can do...and may do many things with this face they is best for them. But what about the one who made me think she is believing herself...I do like her, and love her. This is the kind that I will be sincere with, as well. Since she is not playing, I will not play. She will know the bitterness she is sobbing for, and I will be rigid with the sight of true fear that I can end but know I cannot. Sounds ornate, but that is because language is attempting here a thing that is beautiful and fantastically wondrous.

Her pussy will smell like another, as if she could be anybody because her pussy is as theirs; and some will have a pussy that is scented specifically and separately from all other creatures but they will have adapted too easily. At the end my cum on her somewhere and her sobs hinting to herself that humiliation is wet and desirable and one day possibly a thing which she chases. Maybe there is piss on her, on me and her. I hold her, but always condescending to, and my wife is brushing her hair telling her that she is so pretty and that she will help her, and the girl is nodding yes and gasping the sobs inhaling but I know the girl-Sarah will think that she doesn't want me to touch the thing again because she knows that it is the sort of thing that has power over me and can make me obsess. She knows this because it is the same thing as her. And I really want to go find one of those believing they are sad ones right now but will end up with metallic frown/smile who will always have a more hospitable mouth to cock than a cunt or asshole. I will still put it in her ass and then her mouth. That is the sort of thing that one does if they like to teach lessons as they teach themselves nothing.

4.

It is nine in the morning and I initially left the bed in order to piss. That is, piss in a toilet. This is quite a frequent occurrence for me, pissing in toilets throughout the night, and the place and situation that follows the pissing is also an occurrence happening nightly. That is the desire for sugar, and sating it afterward. When my sister was visiting she would assault me with questions every time I was in the kitchen eating in between sleeping. She thinks that perhaps I am a diabetic, and that maybe my attacks that I have been getting are a result from it. My mom thinks that to be a possibility, but she leans more toward me having the same heart syndrome that she once suffered called P.A.T., or something of the sort seeing she often makes mistakes with such terms, but probably that is what it is called. My mom's comfort was that although you feel that your heart is going to explode and sweat is dripping in puddles down your mouth, cannot move, cannot talk, you do not have to worry about dying in the midst of an attack. That is pleasant to hear but she knows that when you are feeling as such, if she was feeling the same thing as I, that logic sounds very illogical. If you were not fearing death at that moment your body would not be doing what it needed to do in order for it to stop, such as the breathing patterns and the positioning of body, what your body is telling you to do and not do. Even your body is biologically fighting death, because it feels a bit near when your heart is pounding with celerity and ethereal shadowed dots superimposed on vertical bleached plane is all that your eyes see. And sweating, as already said, though I am simply fucking freezing. After the attacks I feel as if I have beguiled, or tricked, manipulated, a thing attempting punishment. But it succeeded. It is just my polarized human mechanism thinking in terms of death=bad, life=good that makes me think that I have the good. Death=bad is just a survival trait that every species that is on this planet today must have to have made it through the evolutionary process. And that is where the genealogy of morals begin, not in terms and uses of language, as someone I love thought. I should return to the cold bed with the warm ass of the monkey girl-Sarah; I like to place my ear on her left nipple and put both my legs through hers.

No, I will suck on her breasts for some time and rub her pussy between her lips through her pajamas and she will begin to shove the whole weight of her little tiny body against that rubbing finger trying to get that thing to slide dryly betwixt her whole damn body cutting in her as a saw in two starting directly from the first connecting part betwixt that jutting cunt and ending at last connection at flesh particles on top of skull. I will have one warm butt-cheek on one side of me with her left body, and her right cheek on my other side with her right body. And I will use the palms of both of my hands to rub left and right pussy concurrently in the same motion, though this time I will rub flat onto fleshy surface with my whole palm and not slide with saw finger lest she and I result in more monkey girl-Sarahs and all her needing to be rubbed pussy parts, but I would blanket myself with all of the sections of warm asses if something tragic such as another severing occurs.

5.

I have to build a big machine within two days. A little boy came up to me today outside of building's door and said to me with the tone of reply "aa-ite, lemmee git dat der."

"Pardon me?," says I.

"wunnadoze der," pointing to a gutter glutted with many possible "those."

So I gave him a cigarette. He took it and jay-ran across the street seemingly continuing in a straight line until my vanishing point, and then he died.

Nothing indicated that that was what he wanted; there was no allusion made to cigarettes by the child. I had to dictate and control what he wanted by choosing to give him whatever I felt he should want. I am still giving, and he is still receiving. Doubly.

6.

The girl-Sarah can be quite the wanker; although, she is the most beautiful wanker. She is damp again. Things can find their way in there quite comfortably now, being wet and concave, you see. I am having a bad time as of late. Really not enjoying much, not that that is the purpose/the goal. Nothing is happening as it should; nothing is happening correctly/properly. I sit and watch it fall down. And it makes no thump as it hits the ground, lies there, huge and defeated. The monkey girl-Sarah, stretched on the bed with back against mattress and head hanging over bottom edge where my toes freeze nude, gazes at it upside down. She may care so much, sobbing somewhere quiet or something, but I don't know. She is a very becoming girl, very pretty and sexy, and stuff.

26

More Journal Entries

9/26/2003

Always dripping. Collective paranoia after day with Sarah. Oh, the way she was crying deepest sadness with vanishing, exquisite whispers. So frightened, she was.

9/28/2003

Everybody may eventually hate me. They always seem as if they like me so much initially, and, for quite some time following. Then they become annoyed and bitter. I leave them alone. It is their hole, their preference for distaste. Yes, I feel bad but it is so random in causal action that there is little I can do to alter their repulsion. Although it seems random in the engendering on my behalf there is a definite phenomena and likeliness for this to occur in my relations to others. Fucking dirty pigs. Ah, all these peasant filled skylines over-gushed to the roots with the ceramic faggot disease. I would want to destroy much and I am tired. The girl-Sarah and all.

She is sleeping because she is tired and because she said she is tired. Yes, I like her. And I'm telling her so and as such. I cannot truly enjoy and appreciate hurting her. The liking of her is so queer. She is such a little-boy-gay and all. Her middle name is Lynn, too. So one could call her Sarah Lynn. I must work today to get money. I am thinking I am a liar and stupid and horrible. Maybe ugly. Also very paranoid. I worry police and those sorts will destroy me somehow so I look out windows a lot to see if they are seeing something or what I am seeing looking at me.

10/01/2003

She really has a dirty face. It does something really dirty.

10/01/03

Always dripping. Collective paranoia after day with Sarah. Oh, the way she was crying deepest sadness with vanishing, exquisite whispers. So frightened, she was. Because Circe was born dominated.

10/04/2003

The days are scary. Really, they are horrifying. The girl-Sarah, and all, makes me see what is horrifying by contrast. I do not enjoy this train. It is humming death everywhere. I do not want that. Not by a train, at least you look at me and you do not think I will burn you. I will burn you sick=face and teeth and everything. Not liking what I see, that is why. I should not tamper with certain things because of my history. What can I do to stop egalitarian-cunt distribution from agonizing the shrink of misery?

10/07/03

I know that Telemachus boy.

10/07/2003

Oh, I can eat them all wonderfully, yes, but the texture is not so nice. It will probably happen a lot, again; that is, fucking the girl-Sarah, monkey, four times between three and eight. It all was nice. I do not care to be rewarded myself by the paradisiacal light. I just would like to be comforted in knowing others will go to hell. Hell is important, heaven is not. Heaven is reactionary to hell. Hell is Prometheus, heaven Epimetheus. Although, I am being reactionary in wanting people to suffer in the autonomous necessary place. The girl-Sarah will be fucked more and much.

10/09/2003

Peasant stuffed substrata. Above it occurs death-bay zenith and penniless-weeping-mother horizon beseeching the goat-smeared future sniffing, running, imploring, apostrophizing powerful daughter's crotch.

10/10/03

Everybody may eventually hate me. They always seem as if they like me so much initially, and, for quite some time following. Then they become annoyed and bitter. I leave them alone. It is their hole, their preference for distaste. Yes, I feel bad but it is so random in causal action that there is little I can do to alter their repulsion. Although it seems random in the engendering on my behalf there is a definite phenomenon and likeliness for this to occur in my relations to others. Fucking dirty pigs. Ah, all these peasant filled skylines over-gushed to the roots with the ceramic faggot disease. I would want to destroy much and I am tired. The girl-Sarah and all. She is sleeping because she is tired and because she said she is tired. Yes, I like her. And I'm telling her so and as such. I cannot truly enjoy and appreciate hurting her. The liking of her is so queer. She is such a little-boy-gay and all. Her middle name is Lynn, too. So one could call her Sarah Lynn. I must work today to get money. Also very paranoid. I worry police and those sorts will destroy me somehow so I look out windows to see if they are seeing something seeing me see them. And if they see something it is perhaps seeing themselves see me by me seeing them only because they see me.

10/12/2003

Thought I was dying today. Heart beating faster that celerity, and the gargantuan-ogre fingertips squeezing my skull possibly attributing to the pointillist paleness of things. They said attack of anxiety. Why would it attack now? I beat it in 30 seconds, maybe.

10/13/2003

We must reform fascism to a comprehensive level. I should probably see a doctor before I die.

10/14/2003

Bataille is making a presumption. I have to read it over. It appears as if he is attributing a negative connotation on his *discontinuous* humans. The gulf between us is ... actually, I thought about it; it is not a negative connotation but rather based on our true patterns of gravitation. Death and eroticism are points of converging, not reproduction but eroticism. Reproduction is creating another *discontinuous* being. Where is the girl Sarah. I want my monkey here now. I did not fuck her yesterday and I am quite certain she will have to today. I will definitely want to put it in her ass. I will not come there if I have not before it gets to watery. I will have to find something else to do with my cock. I wonder about this man who wants to see Sarah and I on Saturday; I do not wonder about him but what I should do- to him, Sarah, ad nauseum. My sister wants me to call her. Mother is a fine human.

10/16/2003

First guards on the deliberate front must be compromised solely of the petite violent muscular black boy; they, who worship those who worship progressive, hyper treachery. Applied with seemingly purposeful, metal control, they will enforce the power's idea.

10/18/03

She really has a dirty face. It does something really dirty. As is Persephone's beauty after the yank down, after the gallop about.

10/18/2003

The girl-Sarah is a thing that touches me much; she is of the frightened alto-whisper glass particle people. There and here, synthesized, lives 6 of them. So as they see, I cannot eat her with ease. The girl-Sarah and I will ascend the flags of the erotofascism betwixt the every air point of the every demos empire. We do not love anything more we exchange. She creates babies so as to be able to easily kill a thing. I am involved with that. I also began enjoying milk. I have not cleaned myself in a few days correctly, but I have every thing else around me. I will not again on this day. I will go to sleep in the beginning and then clean at the time before the end. I do not smell. All always say I do not smell. It is the Wandering Arab Skin mechanicalizing the evolved corrosion of the ill-frown-face weeping Westerner (INFIDELSOONDEATH), of his drooping genitals drippings, into the abundance of our poppy flower scenting pretty faggots.

10/20/2003

Monkey-Sarah has the posture that is queerest. And this girl flitted away from here with this face that has eyes that are round and narcotiqued with those smallest invisible dead liliputs swimming efferent from their distributor...hardest pupil. And the face was softest that it will not break if stepped on, but rather compact and indented while face materiel surrounding that foot crushing expands and rises due to face flesh displacement. Her back went and connected straight to her butt and her butt was shoved out much. It was so much shoved out. And not very big at all. She was such a receptacle for a thing as a stick that I wanted to give her a stick to receive immediately at once. I let the fascist princess hear all the information too. She did not see the girl's butt, though. She saw only malleable face to desire to hug and not butt to receive sticks. I let that girl-Sarah understand that. She should have to consent to me being a deliverer of sticks to such a girl, and if so, possibly, such girls.

10/27/2003

The days are scary. Really, they are horrifying. The girl-Sarah, and all, makes me see what is horrifying by contrast. I do not enjoy this train. It is humming death everywhere. I do not want that. Not by a train. At least you look at me and you do not think I will burn you. I will burn you sick-face and teeth and everything. Not liking what I see, that is why. I should not tamper with certain things because of my history. What can I do to stop egalitarian-cunt distribution from aggravating the shrink of misery?

11/02/2003

Oh, I can eat them all wonderfully, yes, but the texture is not so nice. It will probably happen a lot, again; that is, touching the girl-Sarah, monkey, four times between three and eight. It all was nice. I do not care to be rewarded myself by the paradisiacal light. I just would like to be comforted in knowing others will go to hell. Hell is important, heaven is not. Heaven is reactionary to hell. Hell is Prometheus, heaven Epimetheus. Although, I am being reactionary in wanting people to suffer in the autonomous necessary place. The girl-Sarah will be touched more and much.

11/11/2003

Peasant stuffed substrata. Above it occurs death-bay zenith and penniless-weeping-mother horizon beseeching the goat-smeared future sniffing, running, imploring, apostrophizing powerful daughter's crotch.

11/18/2003

Thought I was dying today. Heart beating faster than celerity and the gargantuan-ogre fingertips squeezing my skull possibly attributing to the pointillist paleness of things. They said attack of anxiety. Why would it attack now? I beat it in 30 seconds, maybe. The souls of thieves even steal.

11/26/2003

We must reform fascism to a comprehensive level. I should probably see a doctor before I die. That is, if they would like to see me sometime. And my pecked liver. Let it grow back once, please and I will bite the fucking bird's head off.

12/03/2003

Bataille is making a presumption. I have to read it over. It appears as if he is attributing a negative connotation on his *discontinuous* humans. The gulf between us is ... actually, I thought about it; it is not a negative connotation but rather based on our true patterns of gravitation. Death and eroticism are points of convergence, reproduction has elements of the erotic in the consciousness of creating death. Reproduction is creating another *discontinuous* being, though. Where is the girl Sarah. I want my monkey here now. I did not sex her yesterday and I am quite certain she will have to today. I wonder about this man who watches the girl-Sarah; but he does not know Sarah, or girl-Sarah, or monkey, or Sarah Lynn, just this thing with brown hair and little boobs. My sister wants me to call her. Mother is a fine human.

12/09/2003

First guards on the deliberate front must be compromised solely of the petite violent muscular black boy; only those who worship those who worship progressive, hyper treachery. Applied with seemingly purposeful, metal control, they will enforce the power's idea.

12/14/2003

The Houses of Atreus are rising again. Rising to bathe the foot of the innocent with the opalescent urine of the squeezed Liar's tongue. It slobbers resourcefully. As it should. The girl-Sarah is a thing that touches me much; she is of the frightened alto-whisper glass particle people. There and here, synthesized, lives 6 of them. So as they see, I cannot eat her with ease. The girl-Sarah and I will ascend the flags of the eroto-fascism betwixt every air point of the every demos empire. We do not love anything more we exchange. She creates babies so as to be able to easily kill a thing. I am involved with that. I also began enjoying milk. I have not cleaned myself in a few days correctly, but I have everything else around me. I will not again on this day. I will go to sleep in the beginning and then clean at the time before the end.

I do not smell. All always say I do not smell. It is the Wandering Arab Skin mechanizing the evolved corrosion of the ill-frown-face weeping Westerner (INFIDELSOONDEATH), of his drooping genitals drippings, into the abundance of our poppy flower scented pretty faggots.

12/27/2003

Monkey-Sarah has the posture that is queerest. And this girl flitted away from here with this face that has eyes that are round and narcotiqued with those smallest invisible dead liliputs swimming efferent from their distributor...hardest pupil. And the face was softest that it will not break if stepped on, but rather compact and indented while face materiel surrounding that foot crushing expands and rises due to face flesh displacement. Her back went and connected straight to her butt and her butt was shoved out much. It was so much shoved out. And not very big at all. She was such a receptacle for a thing as a stick that I wanted to give her a stick to receive immediately at once. I let the fascist princess hear all the information, too. She did not see the girl's butt, though. She saw only malleable face to desire to hug and not butt to receive sticks. I let that girl-Sarah understand that. She should have to consent to me being a deliverer of sticks to such a girl, and if so, possibly, such girls.

1/04/04

Eros will only survive as a boy- bitter, gray, and pretty. But in winter- gay and dizzy. He hasn't wandered on his own for some thousands of years. He is commanded and whored about. He has been tricked by the nihilist with knives. She knew her name. That is how. She knew her pretty little name. Hagl Strid for the bored.

1/10/04

Death is Western. And Japanese. But Japan knows Death's genitalia, and the West doesn't even know their own. Assume definite form of stomps striding past amorphous dragging man, slobbering body into skull banging walls with his crooked leans. Ignore him. Hate him. Kick him, even If your should face kiss one tragedy Eponine will embrace bullets for you.

4/02/2004

I sense patterns. A pattern of recent narrative language, which attempts less language, well, an autonomous less language not literally less language. It may not be truly less language than before, meaning it could actually be more wordy, but it shall feel terse. Possibly not. But that is just one pattern out of many suspected. The literal objectification of death and sex, and only recognizing youth as valid existence. Youth shall always be victorious and immortal over the mortal adult who is conscious of death and time, and their relation to one another. Consciousness of death is the birth of time for the self and the definitive death of youth. It is a death of youth, and not a vanishing because of the manner in which we stare back at adolescence, as a thing once alive, felt, now only existing in the realm of mnemonic whispering, giggling pubescent ghosts. I am too awake, my hyper wide eyed sobriety has pulled the death blanket over the eyes of my ghosts for a last time. They are okay, and I have to suffer and live without them. As long as everybody else has their ghosts to step in front of their eyes to distort and fog things harsh and stark, even if I have to see them and their ghosts doing this, they will never see me naked and real.

4/07/2004

How will we ever know Hugo's France? I mean I see it
though it is severely affected. I utterly feel it, God knows I do,
but as it is seemingly such romanticism of crime, revolution,
is it anymore than today's, and yesterday's, supposed stark
realism? Genet, who actually is supposed to be credible to
speak about prisons and its happenings more than a Camus,
may speak of realistic situations in prison but it is the same
goings on typical of that society then as it is now. Of course
his situations between characters is wholly separate and individually distinct, but it does not mean that what he has to say
generally about anything loses its generality because he has
been intimate with it. It can be as such, and it also may not.
Genet was concerned with certain situations and had a personal aesthetic as does any artist/human. A person detached
and separate from what he speaks of may be much more
revealing than an insider, and that does not need divulging
because it is facile enough. Lord, Genet has such flowery
prose, prosaic prose in some of his literature that you are
suddenly engulfed with damp rosy scented air and colorful
banners with various flora flanking you as you lazily saunter
on a hand-laid stone path with fingers loosely entwined with
your new younger lover who is staring at the side of your face
waiting for your attention. This is fine, but remember that
this is a prison where conditions are obscene and dire. So it
is even more beautiful seeing that he is not purely a spectator
jotting down a photo that his eyes have not even seen before
taking the shot, because even a photo, once your eyes choose
what will be in the frame, is subjective.

4/12/2004

I do things as if I love them and want to kill myself intently. The girl-Sarah is reading what appears as an old red cloth-bound book; I think it may be Brothers' Grimm. I ask her. It is. I need to sleep well and regard other tasks so that I may be able to write as a boy does. I cannot keep my eyelids from closing shut. And I will never be as Ulysses. I need to parody sleep.

27

In His Hand

To the Reader:
When sending money send only postal money orders, bank drafts, or cashiers check. Send no personal checks, payroll checks, or cash. Do not send packages for delivery to inmate.

CHECKS AND MONEY ORDERS MUST BE MADE PAYABLE TO INMATE INDICATING FULL NAME AND INSTITUTION REGISTER NUMBER.

Register Number

Name

Street

City   State   Zip

Name of Sender
Box 99
Pontiac, Illinois 61764

Date

This is not misery. Misery has substance; gives you enough comfortability to be able to view your misery and absorb it. This place descends our post-consciousness to instinct — All you can think of is get me the fuck out so I can just be miserable. After a long, not exactly linear path of stages, each one more abject than the former, it seems and feels as if nothing good can happen again. Ever.

Delicate flower
fragile , tender
skin porcelin
pores glazed
flesh pure
         .innocent.

in a scent
ethereal , edible
    drenched
      lips
heaven intraveneous
   angellic
        Heroin.

   you
little thing
feline , feminine
   with
hypnotic trance inducing worshipme begme
youneedme Mysterium tremendum Igota secret
   cemented
    fixed
   Nucleus
   EYES.

So   utterly
aware ; awake.
cocaine conscious.
Every   thing
    is
mechanical —
   desire
   shitting
   thinking
   breathing
   dying
   rotting
   nothing;
what wretchedness
   to be
enslaved to
every thing;
what wretchedness
   to
know it.
only chaos
   is
freedom , but
if it realized —
it is not
chaos, how horrible human.

Significant → act. 5
A.M.
Seg.

Auto-estrangement (solid moods)

There is a schism that exists in me, that IS me; A greater schism and lesser schisms, like an earthquake's fault line and fissure cracks that form around it as if it is the nucleus. I identify more with the negative emptiness that is the division rather than the objects/things being divided. I do not feel "here". And because I am not "there", I cannot feel "there". If I was there, I would feel "there". Too many illusions/delusions depleted. I need them, but I would have to feign for them to remain. I try, but it does not last long. And I am hungry. Not all of "I"; but a mechanism in "I". It becomes master when it says "feed me" • it makes me shake physically • Different mechanisms do it at different times. Some can be nourished and some's hunger compounds upon feeding, immediately. The ones that can be nourished easily I don't mind; they give me that reward of completion, although I know it is a microcosmic prelude to something else. There is no such thing as movement to any definitive purpose/goal. I just move. Nothingness seems real because I cannot know it. what I understand and conceptualize I know is utterly human and arbitrary bullshit, Vagueness and abstraction to an incomprehensible point suggest purity/truth. Purity/truth is nothing without the human value system ,so…. whatever. Idealistically appealing though,purity/truth, though, then what—if realized. Human, blind vitality breeds languor. ~~⬤~~ Only ~~to~~ those ~~who~~ would rather be sedated and etiolated. ~~There is nothing~~ we can do but ~~pretend~~ ~~there~~ there is purpose, such as writing ~~shit like this.~~ Being inert is logical. ~~⬤~~ We are not allowed to stay inert due to the human condition; i.e., all ~~things~~ the things we are enslaved to (gravity, digestion, sleep, consciousness, eating, dying). So ~~much~~ everything for nothing. Too many objects ~~pushes one~~ induces to stolidity. Stolidity does not exist as a physical manifestation though. Idealistically appealing though. It is too easy to survive; it should occupy more time ~~and~~ and be a struggle just to live. The more we figure out ways to make it easier, it should become harder in proportion to our evolution. It is too ~~easy~~ being human. Diatribes would no longer [It is too easy to write this.] ~~exist. Intellect~~ ~~focused~~ would be focused on survival ~~diminishing existential~~ suffering. Suffering is the birth and apex of consciousness after and before nothingness. Too much ~~involution~~/intricacy. It goes where. ~~Dichotomatic~~ [Dichotomatic] ~~synthesis~~ synthesis /explicit misery / whores -slaves - sycophancy /rhythmic induced nausea -narcissistic mavomania / beckoning paralysis/ hollow dick: arbitrator between cum and acrid pit/another ~~whore /another~~ /vessel ~~flesh~~ / limp - listless /dangling /spit.

It is Sunday. I go to
Surgery Tuesday.
THEY SAY it will
be very complicated
Funny I write
this, you
Know what till I
Cannot think and am not
sure tragedy.

Sanner Al Sheikh
Date ?
Surgery in a few
days

I am surprised this conceit
made itself known to actually
write. I did not know I ~~could~~
could cry to myself like that about
myself. Who really knows how
much of everything is entrapment,
not independent ~~decisions~~
DECISIONS.
they say I could die but I don't know

REMEMBRANCES

Viola May 2006

I remember one day sitting on Samer's couch and looking at one of his tattoos. I asked him about it. He gave me a brief explanation, hinting at mysterious past adventures, and then said, "I'll tell you more about it sometime." So suddenly it hit me. I crumpled to the floor and wept more than I had allowed myself to weep over the past few days. I thought, "I want to ask him to tell me more, but I can't."

And just as suddenly, any and all earthly matters revolving around Samer dissolved into nothing, leaving only the feeling of his spirit – the way Samer made me feel when he was around. Samer's eyes always smiled at me. There was a warmth in him that was otherworldly. He had this way of welcoming one into the fold, so to speak – making one feel acknowledged and exceptional. There seemed to always be that hint of a secret wink in his manner like we were in on the same joke.

[There was something else, too, that is harder to pinpoint. The word chivalrous comes to mind.]

In a strange way, I could have a conversation with Samer without speaking. He would read my gestures and brief words without misunderstanding me. There were never any awkward pauses where I was expected to say something just to say it. I could be myself. There were times that he would even say it out loud, nodding his head: "I know you." This was more reassuring than presumptuous because I felt that he really did care to understand me.

I want to remember and celebrate Samer as a whole. Samer told me once that he would always defend me and my artwork and all that I do. He was fiercely autonomous and respected my autonomy, too. Because of that, I don't want to be too careful or appropriate in my remembrance. I believe that we shared the notion that common propriety and protocol had little to do with the real stuff of life – that the truth and sincerity of your heart is so much more important. That is what I remember.

A few times, we communicated via the written word – the space in which I'm most comfortable. During those exchanges, and while listening to his lengthy discussions with my husband, I got a real sense of his core – his life philosophy, his moral self. Beyond his natural charm, this is what made me respect him most. Samer seemed to have an understanding of something very essential and wise. He saw that there was nothing incongruous between the sensual/erotic and spiritual/religious. He didn't see it as a clash but a symbiosis, or perhaps all facets of the same awesome organism of the soul. I truly feel that he could sense the nature of "God" and, in his best moments, was completely in sync with that. (I think that even in his very worst moments, that reverence was never out of reach.)

Samer, if one can say nothing else about him, left an indelible impression. Over the past few years, I've been writing a story, with one of the central characters inspired by Samer. I never told him this. I could never finish the story because Usama and my relationship with Samer had so many ups and downs. At times the character was the handsome and seductive anti-hero, and at times he morphed into something more grim and poisonous and then back again. So many times I had to write and rewrite this character. Only now do I clearly understand what I'm writing.

Samer's own writing, bits of which I had the privilege of reading here and there, is completely original, and I think it will leave an equally unforgettable impression. I look forward to helping give it to the world. I love you, Samer, and miss you too much. I know that the images you have fashioned through language will render your memory immortal.

Viola Voltairine
Samer's Sister-in-Law

Porochista May 2006

Everyone who's known Samer Alshaibi well in the last few years maybe had expected to get the call I did yesterday. He was one of those people. Larger than life, too much for this world, etc, as the cliches go. Because you knew all that, maybe that was why you told yourself, it could never happen, we'd all go before him. And yet who can argue with the politics of heaven and hell, angel and man.

I first met Samer and Sarah at a photo shoot Kristie [now Viola] was doing on their roof. I was assisting--it was me and three naked Ohioans on a particularly hot July day. Samer and Sarah were busy doing god knows what but Samer kept bringing up water on the roof for us. I had seen photos of both of them before at Usama's: he with his incredible tattoos and childlike eyes and magnetic charisma, her with her beauty and braces and otherworldly poise. I was spellbound by their spirit.

A week later, I was walking my old sick greyhound on my block, which was only a block over from theirs. Samer had seen me and called after me. I was amazed they remembered me. Sarah immediately rushed to King, my dog, and sat on the concrete with her face buried in his bony ribs. They asked me questions, they cared about my life, they said they wanted to see me.

For the next several months or so, I saw them all the time. They were my new Chicago family.

Every single night of our time together they walked me home. Samer, no matter where we were, nevermind they lived a block over, would walk me home and walk with me while I walked my dog. (King loved them. Samer had a way of scratching his ear that would make his legs twitch ecstatically--I could never recreate it.) They always checked in. He was often the first person I spoke to and the last.

They would take me out to dinner. MOD, this great place where Muslim cabbies would go late at night, the best diner in the east village, that hookah bar. Wherever we went, Sarah and I would take our time with the menus and in the end Samer would order for us. When it came to his meal, he would make numerous modifications and ask endless questions. The waiters were very patient but he'd win them over with that charm, that smile and that voice.

He had the best voice. Always charged and enthused, incredibly boyish, even infused with a sort of natural hip. You could imagine him, a wisecracking teen of the Tompkins Square squat or the numerous other settings of his incredible lifelong adventures. . .

Sarah was the light of his life, his wife, his muse, his everything. We'd spend entire afternoons in front of Sarah talking about her in the third person. We both decided she needed to go platinum blonde. (Sarah, up for anything, brave girl that she was, would shrug and say fine.) Then Samer and I would flip through fashion magazines and discuss models and the season and all sorts of girl crap that it was amazing to watch this big, strong, muscular, heavily-tatted tough guy who had been to prison go on and on about. He was the most secure person in the world.

He would make fun of Sarah and my laziness. He was constantly trying to teach us "how to run." Stretches to do. He told me once I had to eat 60 grams of protein after I ran or else all that exercise that could go to muscle, would go to waste. He would get mad if I didn't.

He had the most amazing taste. Anyone who has been to Samer and Sarah's can attest to this. The apartment had the feel of a 1930s saloon, baroque, subversive, gothic, a bit decaying, with bits of

middle eastern influence here and there. The aesthetic penetrated every inch. None of it came out of money but great taste. He would let you know--he was very proud of his perfect eye.

When it was time for me to leave Chicago, he said he wanted to throw a going away party for me at his apartment. We invited everyone I knew, from my mom who was in town, to my dog, to all sorts of Wicker Park kids. From the beginning Samer took the reins. He ordered all sorts of upscale Middle Eastern eats paired with all sorts of fabulous alcohol and although he didn't drink, he made everyone amazing cocktails. Even my mother, who was in town.

He was amazing to my mother. My mother who wouldn't even sit next to a teenage girl with a lip ring, was suddenly constantly lost in conversation with this chain-smoking punk rock boy day and night. He told her she was like a second mom. He told her she was beautiful over

and over.

Samer had a way with women. Sarah was his muse and

a model, but he seemed to also want every woman to be a model. He would tell me I should. I would look at him and roll my eyes. He would snap at me to stop it--eventually I would find myself saying, fine, you're right,

um, yeah, I'm gorgeous. He could make you agree to anything.

When I left Chicago they not only came to the airport to see me and my dog off, they came with presents, a lovely Halston top and a Lacoste shirt I had wanted for ages. All I left them with was the rubble of my apartment. . .a lease I was running away from, an apartment I was basically abandoning without packing a single item. I told them they could have anything. It was all crap, but Samer, because he was polite, I knew, acted like it was a bunch of nice stuff. We both knew better, but I appreciated it.

The next time I saw him was on election day in Chicago a year and a half ago--I was visiting this time. We sat around the TV and watched Kerry lose. As always, he was impeccably dressed, calm, and articulate, while we were in shit clothes, drunk, pissed, and loud. He seemed happy. He said he had a lot of plans for his business. I couldn't help but think he felt betrayed by me for leaving Chicago. Samer never ever guilt-tripped anyone, but if you ever sold him short, not even intentionally, you felt it. Most likely he felt you feel it and just let you. He was that cool.

I'm sad I didn't give half as much as he gave me. I should have helped some more with the clothing store he wanted to open--but try explaining to Samer that no one on earth knows more than he does about his very particular interests. What could I do? With Samer, I should have realized it was about family, community, creating your own world. I wasn't good enough to get this.

I also regret not showing him my writing and reading more of his. We were supposed to do this, but I would shy away every time. I wish I knew what he would have thought. More than anything Samer's love was writing, his whole soul was that of a writer.

I read over all his long, labyrinthic, beautiful emails. He writes the emails writers do. They were always full, long, too much, mysterious, mischievous, brilliant, dumbfounding. They were never self-absorbed though, unlike most writers. His emails were often more about you than himself. He called me "little banana", "dark lips." "Miss madness." Every email had the reassurance that he would always be there, he was never going anywhere.

Like I told Sarah on the phone, last night, the night he died, his was an energy that could never be lost. He would come back from the dead to tell you that. I wish he would. I can't imagine a better spirit dead, like I couldn't imagine a better spirit alive.

xxxx p
Porochista Khakpour
Samer's friend

Usama May 2006

It has been over a week and Samer's death is still resounding heavy in me. But the sensation is pleasant. I feel my brother's passion in the air. With a razor tongue, and eyes of angels, Samer was filled with an intensity and fire that will never stop burning. He is in all of us. He reminds me of my past, of our religion, of God. Samer is light and dark swirling all over his shadow and words. How can I say anything?

I felt his peace as he departed. In some half-waking dream, I embraced him, and we kissed Iraqi style, and we said goodbye. I remember how his coffin was in front of all the men kneeling in prayer. He would have liked that.

His body lies in peace and with God.

Please remember his spirit and smile with love and enjoy this brief beautiful life.

Usama Alshaibi
Samer's Older Brother

More Memories

For notes and images posted by friends and family of Samer, go to:
https://remembersamer.blogspot.com/